THE
BONE
YARD

THE BONE YARD

GARY YOUNG

KETOS PRESS

This book is dedicated to
Richard

FOREWORD

by Phil Cousineau

"The past is not dead; it's not even past," is one of the most haunting lines in twentieth-century literature. Taken from William Faulkner's novel, *Requiem for a Nun*, the words have the power of a defiant aphorism, the urgency of a cautionary tale.

At the heart of Gary Young's novel, *The Boneyard*, is a rhapsody on a theme of the existential problem about time and memory, which he presents as a conundrum: What is it that can be dug up but can also bury us?

To which he replies: a secret.

If we dare to dredge up the past, he says, we need to be prepared for the consequences. If we don't, we are condemned to repeat what we were ill-advised to forget.

"My story wrestles with secrecy on more than one level," Young has written elsewhere, "If there is a peaceful village, you can be sure that a rabid wolf is in the woodlands." His book is rife with such echoes of folklore, the danger lurking in the dark forest and in the human heartland.

As revealed in the author's Preface, the story is inspired by a boyhood memory that has bulldogged him and never let him go. The author's cousin revealed to him a family legend about bodies that were buried in the barnyard of their great uncle's farm in the Missouri valley. According to his cousin, rumor had it that the site contained the bones of bushwhackers who had been masquerading as members of the Confederate Army in the days when they were attacking local German farmers from the Rhineland. The immigrant's violent reckoning with the varmints, in the parlance of the day, was so grievous that "necessity mandated a secret," and both their actions and reactions reverberated over several generations.

But those are only the bare bones, if you will, of the legend, which needed to be fleshed out to have the heft of a compelling narrative that could talk to us today.

This task is borne out by what Young has described as "an insistence in reconstructing the past." To my mind, these references to the puissant powers of necessity are a reminder of the personification of the force known in classical times as Ananke, one of the most powerful and most feared of all goddesses. This constant presence in the human adventure may account for what his remark about what having encounters with "mythical spirits" while composing the book.

Thus emboldened, he responded to the desire to "write down the country," as the French adventurer René Caillié memorably described his own inner directive to record his impressions about the forbidden world of Timbuktu.

Where does this irrepressible impulse come from?

After writing professionally for over fifty years, I am still in awe of the urge and the devotion to the practice. I am reminded of my father's encouragement of my writing ambition, saying to me that we die twice, once when our heart gives out, and then again when people stop telling stories about us.

"Write," he insisted, "so the world will remember you and what you have been fortunate—or unfortunate—enough to encounter."

Every bona fide storyteller feels that compulsion in their gut. It is clear on every page of Young's book that he is driven to preserve even a fragment of the world he grew up in, so the world might not forget those times and places. But his efforts get to the essence of the word, which comes from the French *recorder*, "to move through the heart."

"I am compelled to tell this story," he writes," so that no one will ever be able to say that the past was a waste or act like it doesn't matter."

The profound depths of this motivation move me deeply because it reveals more than an author's ego speaking. If you listen intently, you will hear the voice of his daemon, which Socrates regarded as our second soul. To plunge into those depths requires more than an historical account of our experiences that inform us. What was called for was nothing less than an alchemy of words distilled in the alembic of the author's imagination.

The Boneyard reflects such a transmutation.

On the surface, the story revolves around two boys in post-war Missouri who are determined to solve a mystery about the boneyard in their own barnyard. But that is merely the Overstory, the plot and nothing but the plot.

The Understory, which is where mythology dwells and psychology lives, turns on several compelling dramatic questions. Can the boys face the ghosts from the past that their curiosity has summoned? What are the consequences of trying to bury the past, as the indelible character of Granma tries to do near the end of the book, declaiming, "Enough! The Civil War is long over." The family matriarch embodies the antediluvian fear of the dead returning to spook us, as well the dangerous grasp of "Holdfast," that monstrous force from myth that returns in every generation determined to prevent change and keep things the same as it ever was.

And yet of all of the themes explored in *The Boneyard*, the one I find most compelling revolves around the moral dilemma facing the young heroes, Richard and Gig, who feel the need to break the ancient code of silence, even it means risking the sin of desecration. To do so requires a belief in a higher loyalty, the truth itself. Young expresses the philosophical truism here with feeling, the telltale sign of strong writing, in the words of literary critic Roger Rosenblatt. What drops the narrative into the archetypal realm is the author's use of an ever moving dramatic tension be-tween violence and catharsis, vengeance and justice, necessity and freedom.

But fear not, dear reader, for his characters are not stand-ins for abstract ideas. The author limns his young heroes as believable and sympathetic, humorous and melancholic, but also as what he has described a "points of light" in a time of thickening darkness.

To make such character transformations convincing requires the ability to create a sense of transport, which is what my friend and colleague Dr. Huston Smith reminded me was the exquisite point of overlap between the artistic and religious impulse, in the experience of the spiritual realities in The Other World.

In doing so, the author transforms a sliver of family lore into a universal tale in a style that reminds me of the initiation tales collected by the Grimm Brothers, the spiritual parables of Frederick Buechner, and the gothic mysteries of John Bellair. I find that making such connections in literature constitute one of the deepest pleasures of the reading life, which is the thrill of discovering a story that reminds us of other stories, other worlds, but whose characters are unique enough to defy comparison and allows them to stand alone, fresh, and vital.

Which is to say that the narrative voice here rings true, the tone feeling alternating between tough and tender. Often while reading the book, I smiled in recognition of a heartfelt response to the age-old question I often pose to myself and students in my writing retreats: "What would disappear forever if you don't write about it?"

Not everyone is moved by the probing of this question, but true storytellers can't live with themselves if they are sensitive to the fugitive nature of the fleeting moment, or the sliver of eternity they experienced and will never forget. To paraphrase William Saroyan, a writer is someone who can't can't write about experiences that have touched their souls or disturbed their imagination.

There are whole worlds clashing in that double negative.

The Boneyard is proof that the telling of tales is a necessity, not an indulgence, even, at times, a moral imperative. There is evidence here reminds us that story-telling is one of our noblest ways of making meaning out of meaninglessness.

The author's generous worldview is amplified by the inclusion of the poem that festoons the back cover of his book, well-hewn verses that give rise to the ancestral spirits of the German immigrant families who ask him across the abyss of time, "Remind me who I am."

While reveling in these verses, I was reminded of one of the last poems written by the great Stanley Kunitz, to Elise, his third wife of forty-six years, which concludes with the shiver-inducing line, "Touch me, tell me who I am."

If this isn't the task of literature, I don't know what is.

To be touched, moved, and reminded that words matter.

Listening to the spirits of our ancestors and the *anima mundi*, the soul of the earth itself, and responding with a story of our own that touches the hearts of our readers, is not just an act of bravura but a bittersweet compulsion to see our lives in context of those who came before us and provide context for those who follow.

Finally, I am reminded, too, of the great Irish poet W. B. Yeats, who wrote in one of the holiest of poems, "Vacillations," that he knew the moment he had crossed a major threshold in his life when he realized he "was blessed and could bless."

These numinous words touch on the generosity of spirit that pervades Gary Young's Proustian search for lost time, and his attempt to redeem it. His efforts have most assuredly not gone to waste. By virtue of the epiphanic ending of his book, I believe the author has followed the hallowed advice of the old-timey preachers and blues singers and sanctified the past.

In doing so, he has helped us recognize what is sacred about our own lives, our own time.

Phil Cousineau
San Francisco, Summer 2020

PREFACE

This is not a true story but there are persons and places very much like the people and their places whom you will meet in this story. Nobody should get the idea that he or she is a character in this book because it doesn't work that way. The idea for this story came to me a long time ago when my cousin Richard passed some information to me that he supposedly heard from another older cousin. Because of that, Richard gets to be a character in this story but don't think that the Richard in this book is like my cousin Richard and, for sure, don't think that Richard's cousin in this book is Gary Young. In other words, step into the story and forget about being a detective outside of it.

THE FAMILY SECRET

Christmas Day at the Bauers always drove anything evil away from the house. Wartime made little difference and 1944 looked like it would be a victorious year, so the happiness seemed increased. Grandma was running around her house making sure all her family was eating the banquet she and the other women prepared. The smell of turkey and seasoning pervaded the house combined with aromas arising from homemade bread rolls, sweet potatoes, white corn, and mashed potatoes, chocolate meringue pies, and German spice cookies. The gathering reflected a typical American family but coloring it was its German Catholic background.

When they spoke about the war on other days, the Bauers wondered about and prayed for their distant relatives in The Rhineland, who were no doubt dodging the bombs the Allies were delivering to the Nazis. "Poor Monika!" Grandma remarked once when listening to the radio. "She can't stand Hitler but she has to take the bombs. Ach du lieber...!"

Some of the family weren't home for Christmas. Albert was somewhere in the South Pacific. His parents were glad he would not be attacking Germans but, of course, they worried about their youngest son. Albert's sisters Mary and Ida were not at home either. They were Benedictine nuns and were only permitted to visit their parents rarely. Wartime restrictions made any visits from them less likely. Like Albert in uniform, their photos were on the piano. Mary (Sister Hildegard as she was called) was dressed in her white garb including the pleated collar and the long white veil. She was a nurse. Ida (Sister Mechtild) wore the same garb ("habit," Grandma said) except most of it was black. She taught grade school way down in Texas. In the photograph, they were standing together, black and white, in front of a picture of a church window. They were smiling which Grandma said they never stopped doing.

Gig's mama was their sister. Her name was Gen for Genevieve. All of the Bauer girls were attractive but Gen Bauer was the loveliest of all as Joseph Schuster never failed to declare. Gig's mama had told her son, when he was younger, that his dad died overseas before America got into the war and that she decided to use her family's name for her and him so that Gig would have a strong family connection. She said that she had no contact with his other grandparents and told Gig that he should consider Grandpa as his father and he should only think of his daddy when he prayed for him at night.

2

There was another aunt for Gig. Philomena was the oldest Bauer daughter but she was the silliest and, even now, she was in the living room showing jitterbug steps to all who would watch. She had married an Irishman from Kansas City and, like Albert, he was in the army and stationed in the Pacific. His name was Tom Fitzpatrick and they had a son Gig's age. His name was Richard. He and Gig were more like brothers than cousins. As Grandma said, they were double mischief but double delight when together. Richard and his mother lived in Kansas City with his dad's parents so Gig was glad to have him home for Christmas. Usually a hundred miles lay between them. Now they were already discussing summer plans.

Gen's oldest brother (Paul) was at the family Christmas. He was a farmer and the President said that farmers were needed at home. He had a wife (Felicia) and four children: Silas (16), Martin (15), Theresa (12) and Philip her twin. Richard and Gig were 10. Uncle Paul's family was always busy at the farm except on Sunday. No work then unless it was emergency. They lived on the farm which had been in the family for generations.

Grandma and Grandpa had moved into town after handing the farm over to Uncle Paul.

Their present house was one of the largest in Wallenhorst, deep inside Missouri. Twice some renamers from the railroad wanted to change the name of the town because it was German. But men from the parish challenged them with common sense and reminded them

that all Germans were not Nazis. The parish was the heart of the town and of the Bauer family. That's the way it was.

That's why it was natural that Father Boniface was at the Christmas party. He was a Benedictine too and when he went "home", he said, it was the monastery in northern Missouri. His family was German but they lived in Nebraska. He was not as old as Grandma and Grandpa but he was older than anyone else at the party and had spent years as the pastor of St. Hilda's in Wallenhorst.

That day he blessed the Christmas Tree with holy water and then all the food. He was the first to get a plate after Grandpa handed him a plain white envelope. Gig knew there was money in it and a card which said "For Personal Use." Like the Benedictine nuns, Father Boniface was usually expected to give his money to his superior at the monastery.

The house was like a noisy factory but the fun was worth the noise. Nearly everyone except the kids had drunk the latest batch of Grandpa's wine. He was flushed like most of his guests and was showing off his new deer rifle. Uncle Paul cautioned him about handling it. "Don't forget what you pulled last Easter when you showed Father your shot gun." Everyone laughed, remembering the blast that opened up the dining room ceiling and brought down plaster in Father's plate. While he laughed, Father Boniface made the gesture of protecting his chocolate pie.

Grandma was scrambling around with bowls and serving plates heedless of the group's demand that she sit down and enjoy herself. "I am enjoying myself," she responded. Every once in awhile, she paused in front of a mirror and adjusted the bun in the back of her head, which Gig considered the symbol of all grandmothers.

Most of the men were in the dining room, lingering over leftovers and swapping stories. Virgil Kempchen, a great story teller and an old bachelor, had arrived for his share of the hospitality and pink wine. Virgil and Gig's grandparents had been young folks together out by Clear Creek and so the family always demanded him to reveal stories about them in their youth. This Christmas was no exception. Philomena (Phil), tired of her dancing, came into the dining room and asked Virgil to tell about her mother's dancing history. "No tales!" Grandma warned her old friend.

Theresa wanted to hear about her grandmother too, so she started a chorus of requests which sent Grandma to the kitchen and set Virgil to digging up the past. He spoke:

"Her daddy, Mister Henry Huber, had to keep an eye on her until Emil Bauer came and took Rose Huber for himself. But you should have been at their wedding dance. Right there in your front yard, Theresa. (Rose Huber (Grandma) inherited that farm from her father and she passed it on to her children, who had decided Paul should work it for them but take most of the profit.)

Virgil continued: "We built a dance floor right there in the front yard." Then he turned to his friend. "Emil remember how you suggested that we build it behind the oldest barn so we could run in just in case it rained? Ha. Ha. You wanted to dance in the boneyard." Gig wondered why Virgil didn't say barnyard.

Grandpa's face clouded. Grandma snapped mysteriously. "No tales!" She gave Virgil a hard look and he sobered from his wine a bit. He switched tracks skillfully then:

"Rose and Emil made that the best wedding for ten years at least. And Rose waltzed best of all. The fiddle couldn't keep up with her. I should know since I was the fiddler. Agnes played the upright piano. It took an army of us to set it under that maple tree. Agnes. Only a year later she was dead and buried." He paused. Grandpa laid his hand on Virgil's arm. "May she rest in peace," Grandpa prayed. Everyone automatically said "Amen."

Later Mama told Gig and Richard that Agnes had been Virgil's fiancee. They would have been married the day of her funeral.

Gig spoke up after the Amen. "Mister Kempchen, why did you say boneyard instead of barnyard?" Grandma rolled her eyes. Virgil twisted his lips like he wanted to say something.

Then, Silas spoke up. "Is there any truth to the story that there's Confederate soldiers buried in that fallow field by the new barn? When Ed Lang was alive, he told me that there's three unmarked graves in that patch." Father Boniface lifted his eyebrows. Gig's eyes, always huge, met Richard's, now competing in size. A silence seemed to have entered the room.

Virgil jumped the tracks. "Rose, your pies get better year after year." She cut him another slice and almost begged him to eat it whole so she could cut him another. "Well,"

Phil spoke, "what have you heard different from Silas?" Virgil shook his head and pointed to his full mouth. Grandma spoke, "Enough! The Civil War is long over and we have something much worse on our hands. Let's say a prayer for our boys. Father?"

The priest took the cue and thanked God for the feast of Christmas and for goodwill, for the hospitality of the Bauers, and for the advances of the Allies. Then he prayed for the safety of Albert and of all service people, including his nephew. After that, he rose to leave, shaking the crumbs from his black habit. All knelt and he gave them his blessing before Grandma handed him a package of food " for later." He left with merry voices in his ears like bells pealing.

During a lull, Gig insisted, " What's the secret about the barnyard?" Grandma replied quite firmly and finally. "Some things are not for discussion." She happened to exchange a glance with Gig's mama and her daughter lowered her eyes as she did occasionally when talking got intense. Phil then grabbed her sister and pulled her into the living room. "Let's jitterbug!" Phil pinched her sister's bottom to make her laugh. "That's right! Dance!" Grandma agreed and then she spoke to her old friend. "Virgil, here's a food package for you too. Thanks for sharing Christmas with us. God bless you!" He left the house shortly after the priest.

When the leaving started, Felicia started gathering her men and her daughter for the ride to Clear Creek, while speaking to the others. "We want you all to visit during the holidays so make it a point to get out there. Maybe we'll build a dance floor for you, Phil. Richard's mother winked at his favorite cousin, who was thinking about something else. "Oh, here's Joe," Felicia continued. "We're making room for you, Joe. We're not running away from you. Merry Christmas, Joe!"

Joe Schuster had come to see Gen. Everyone knew that including Gig. And it was nice to see her blush when he handed her a little gift in those massive hands. He too was a farmer and just a bit old for military service. Everyone liked Joe but especially Gen.

"I wondered if you 'd care to ride to Highland with me, Gen, to drop my gift off at Aunt Sophie's. We wouldn't be gone long." Gen looked around the living room.

"Gig, get your mama's coat!" Aunt Phil ordered. And he ran upstairs to her room to get it. Soon the couple was gone. His aunt helped her mother put the final touches of cleanliness to the house. Both Grandpa and Grandma were drowsy and their remaining daughter urged them to go to bed. "I'll put the boys away and you two get yourselves to bed too. You laid out a good Christmas and now you need a rest. I'll wait up for Gen and listen to some Christmas music on the radio. I need some time alone." She wanted to write to Tom.

Richard had been arranging a battle for toy soldiers from a set called The Blue and The Gray. Gig squinted at the arrangement as if to suggest a rearrangement but his aunt clapped and that meant bedtime. Each brushed his teeth, peed, and then put on flannels. They shared Gig's bed, which was in the unheated upstairs. Philomena slept with her sister during her visit and they had the upper bedroom closest to the stairs. Quick prayers. A sprinkle of holy water from Grandma and the boys were ready to get their cold feet in a warm feather bed.

Christmas night settled over the house and the village like a setting hen warming her eggs. Inside the Bauer house, the only noise was the scratching of Phil's pen telling Tom of the good time his in-laws shared. She smiled during most of her writing except when some soft radio music stressed the intense awareness of separation. When she was just about ready to conclude the letter, a woman's voice sang, "Sentimental Journey" and Phil bawled quietly when she wrote "Love and kisses, Phil." For all of her silliness, Phil was no less deep than her sisters in the convent. Their hearts and their humor were much quieter than Phil's but all of the Bauers shared the awareness of Life's importance including its demands and rewards. Phil rose when her sister returned and warmed her with a shot of precious bourbon and a barrage of questions about romance. Before long, Phil and Gen joined the silent song of peaceful slumber, which held at bay shadows near and far.

THREE GRAVES

Gig's real name was Greg or Gregory. But when he was learning to talk, he couldn't say Greg without pronouncing it as Gig. The mispronunciation stayed. He figured "Gig" was different but he couldn't really say why. Of course, he didn't know this feeling was usual among kids who were "different."

When Richard and he hopped into bed, they only had a brief conversation before they drifted away to other places. Naturally they were both interested in the boneyard topic and promised one another to find out more about it when summer came and Richard could spend a longer time in Wallenhorst. Just as the height of their plans were in place, sleep took them. Gig halfway heard his mother come up the stairs with his Aunt Phil and heard their low murmurs for awhile but darkness pulled him away again.

Gig became a spectator that night. It was though a large movie screen was before him and he saw everything in great detail. He saw Uncle Paul's house coming to him from a distance. It was brand new and against a cloudy sky. Some things were missing from the yard it seemed. He saw a boy who looked very much like himself running toward the house like he was scared. The boy was bare-footed and wearing rough, old-fashioned clothing. Gig heard an older man's voice say, " Vhat bothers Henry?"

A couple were standing at the back door of the house and both of them were dressed like the relatives seen in albums. They were obviously the boy's parents and their faces were worried. "The boy seems frightened--as though a ghost is pursuing him," the lady said. Her husband put his arm around her waist automatically as if to reassure her.

"Bushvhackers! Bushvhackers!" the boy cried. "Bush-vhackers!" he shouted again when he regained more of his breath. "They're coming here, Fader!" His mother caught him and sat next to him on the grass.

"The horses." The man spoke. "They're after the horses!" He looked at the boy. "Henry, take the horses to the high ridge near the deer blind. Stay vith them until one of the family comes for you. Go now!"

Henry's brother Clement had come from the barn and heard and he spoke up. "Keep Henry here, Fader! They won't mess with a boy. I'll take the horses to the ridge and he was bareback astride Thunder in the same breath. His mother had opened the gate and was shooing the horses after Thunder with a shake of her apron. The rest of the horses followed Clement across the pastures and towards the woodland.

"Mutter, take the girls and hide in the chicken house. Now!" The girls had come out of the house at the sound of the horses heading out. A cloud of road dust was getting closer. Clement and the horses were just inside the woods. The chickens fluttered with excitement when the mother and her daughters swished their skirts among them and then ducked inside the low house to peer out from the cracks in the boards. The chickens seemed to share the danger and cooperated like the horses did. Except for some hens, the rest scratched the yard.

There was a good wind which blew any dust away which had arisen with Clement's rush. Henry's father threw down his hoe beside the cistern. "Say nothing, Henry, unless I speak to you."

A trio of horsemen rode into the yard between the house and the barn. They and their horses were caked in dust streaked with running sweat. The men and horses had angry eyes and greedy mouths.

"Good day," spoke the farmer.

"Horses! We need horses for Belle Starr!"

"I have vater for you and your horses. Henry, pump vater!"

"I SAID WE NEED HORSES!" yelled the man who seemed to be the leader. He and his two companions hopped onto the ground. One of them headed for the house; the other for the chicken yard. The leader faced the farmer.

"Look, Kraut, I want horses or I burn this farm. I'm here from Belle Starr. Help the cause or else!" Belle Starr and her gang presented themselves as Confederate patriots but they were mostly thieves. The German had heard of her and her henchmen. They were called bushwhackers because they were cowardly and made innocent folk their victims more than Union soldiers.

The horses are in a far pasture today," the farmer responded. "You will have to wait a few hours until I can get word to my boy." His voice pitched a little when on the thieves almost stuck his head into the chicken house. A wildly barking dog distracted all of them however. The dog was Henry's and he was upset about the man rifling through the kitchen. Out came the man, harried by the dog, carrying a sack of freshly baked bread, a small ham, and a large bottle of beer. That robber called to his partner in the chicken yard to join him in the house and to bring their saddle bags.

"Do you mean to tell me that you have not one horse in the pen right now? Kraut! Do you expect me to believe you?"

"You think vat you have to think," Henry's father said. "But you vill find no horses here."

The other robbers were breaking and slamming things in the kitchen. The owner placed a heavy hand on his son's shoulder to restrain him. The shadows inside the chicken house remained calm. The leader was splashing buckets of water on his heated horses. Henry pumped quickly after his father's second bidding.

The brutes came out of the house with most edible booty. "More weight for tired horses!" the boss complained. The men dropped their bags and the three of them menaced the farmer. Henry kept cranking the cistern handle. He hoped he would distract them with his activity.

The boss produced a gun as did the men with him. They waved the guns in the air first. Henry froze. His father told him to sit down by the cistern.

"Vill you shoot a man because he has no horses?"

"You're lying!" the bushwhackers said in unison.

"The horses are far!" shouted Henry.

"Like their women," muttered the youngest thief.

"How far?" asked the boss.

"If I run there, it may take 3 or 4 hours to herd them and bring them back."

"Damn! " the leader cursed. "Damn!"

The silence then was loud. The farmer told his son to go find the horses. "Now!" he punctuated. Henry headed into the direction opposite of Clement's. "Such smart sons," thought their father. Henry ran into the field behind the barn and then ran for awhile parallel to the fence until he knew he was out of sight. He then crawled back through tall pokeweed and lush grass toward the sound of the angry voices.

Henry used to hide in that pokeweed patch when his father was ready to whip him. Now he could see his father, still pressed and threatened by the three angry figures. Then, Henry found that he was not alone in the patch. His eyes met Otto Schlotzhauer's and then they met the one eye of his hunting rifle. Otto winked at him, using his mummed lips to ask for stillness.

Shortly, Henry and Otto heard something hair raising:

"For your failure to support the Confederate States of America, I order your execution."

The three marauders faced the farmer and braced themselves taking aim.

Shots rang out and Henry's mother ran out of hiding followed by her two screaming daughters. What they found however was not a dead husband but the corpses of their enemies. Each of them had a head wound, as though their killers had been within a few inches of them. In seconds, five young Germans, not counting Henry, emerged from the thicket across the road, from the barn shadows, and from the shade of a healthy maple tree near the barnyard. They had fired from three positions with obvious precision and accuracy.

"Gott. Gott." sighed the farmer. There was no exaltation. Henry's mother made the sign of the cross over the bodies, while the girls screamed again and ran into their house--terrified of the blood and the deaths. Actually, there was not much blood. The scene was as clean as a deer hunt. Each of the shooters came up to the farmer and received his handshake. "Otto. Martin.

Leo. Hermann. Wilfrid. Thanks! Thanks!"

"Will there be more of them?" the wife cried.

"Perhaps," answered Otto.

"We must bury these now." the farmer said. He headed for a wood shed. It was mostly empty because winter wood had not yet been cut. Henry's father set the five youths to digging three graves in the dirt floor of the shed. His mother went into the house to calm the girls by getting them to clean the kitchen.

As the farmer gathered his wits, he called Otto out of the shed and sent Henry in his place. "Take their horses to Clement on the high ridge and stay with him until nightfall. If you see a lighted lantern in the kitchen window, come in the house. It should be safe. One of us can ride back and fetch Clement and the rest of the horses."

In less than thirty minutes, the men dragged the bodies to the shed and covered them in their graves. Henry shooed his dog away while he splashed water on the bloody spots in the yard. His mother had emptied the saddle bags and returned her goods to their proper places.

The girls were sent to gather berries. Atop the graves, the men scattered pieces of firewood to camouflage the tomb. Henry's father latched the door securely and said, "Now we must build a new voodshed."

Their guns and ammunition were buried with their owners. "I will sell the horses and tack and give the money to the new priest. I vant nothing of theirs to remind us. Ve vill eat supper vhen Clement and Otto return. Henry, get a lantern ready for the kitchen vindow."

Evening was not far off.

Otto saw the lighted lantern after sunset, came into the house to fetch it, and then he waved it vigorously toward the hills after jumping on the chicken house. Of course, the fowl complained. The sound of several horses coming told the hungry children that supper would be ready. Although they weren't starved, they knew that food makes a good distraction. The older portion of the group ate lightly: some wine, some bread, some cheese, some blackberries. No meat. The girls went to bed early after their mother sprinkled them with holy water and recited a few prayers with them.

"I was hunting when I saw Henry throw down his fishing pole to race home."

"They were watering their horses at the ford. They looked mean and they were so upset they didn't notice me."

"You are a good son, Henry. You saved us the grief that could have been. Your mutter and I are proud of you. Otto, how did you gather your army?" There was a needed laughing.

"The others were haying, as I should have been, so I knew where to find them. In these times, we keep our rifles under the hay. And we took our positions after we planned our action in the poke patch."

"So, Henry is not the only one to use the patch for hiding," the mother said. Henry looked innocently at the ceiling. There was more soft laughter.

Then the farmer grew stern. He stood and faced his family and young friends:

"Ve could boast about today. I could boast about the brave vomen and the brave men. You could boast about your marksmanship. And I could boast about my deliverance. But I vant your solemn promise that you vill never speak of this again even among ourselves. Mutter, tomorrow you vill speak vith the girls too. Bloodshed brings vith it sorrow although today's killing vas necessary. Those men brought violence on my farm and it turned against them.I pray to Gott it vill leave us now. Ve must not encourage it to stay by speaking of it. Ever." All nodded, even the boy Henry.

The farmer continued. "You boys tell your parents that you vere helping me vith my horses. The matter began vith horses. Ve shall end it vith horses. Now, go home and Gott be vith you. Tell your families I am sorry for having delayed you. I don't vant you to lie to them but, knowing young men, I know you can make good excuses." He smiled.

Henry's mother spoke. "You have saved my husband and, therefore, my family's life. If any of you ever need anything, I am your servant."

As the young men left, each patted Henry's head. Otto winked at him as he did in the weed patch earlier. The farmer walked with them to the road and then Henry and Clement watched their father sprinkle the woodshed with what must have been holy water. When he came back into the house, the farmer told his sons to sleep in peace.

When he awoke, Gig had forgotten most of his dream but he remembered that something violent had happened on the family farm. He was distracted, however, by breakfast and another day with his cousin. Christmas vacation with Richard was too short to be preoccupied with just one adventure.

THE FALLOW FIELD

"Fallow. F-a-l-l-o-w. Fallow. Untilled. Unsown. Fallow."

"Now use it in a sentence," Gig's grandfather commanded.

"Sister never makes us do that," Gig replied.

"I'll have to talk to her about that. What's the use of learning words if you can't use them? Your vocabulary is fallow!"

"Bravo, Dad!" Gig's mother called from the kitchen. "And we all know whose mouth is never fallow," she added.

Everybody laughed. The vocabulary exercises continued in the living room while the women cleared supper leavings and checked the pantry for the next day's meals, speaking low.

"Mom, Gig is so lucky to have Dad. I wonder if he ever considers himself deprived of a father."

"We're going to need more vanilla when the Watkins Man comes by again," her mother said, but Gen knew that she was paying attention.

" One of these days I'm going to have to tell him that his dad did not die overseas. If he was a dull-witted kid, I wouldn't worry so much but he asks so many questions. You know he does. His brain isn't fallow," she laughed.

"Gen, let sleeping dogs lie. Randy Bell has a wife and daughter now and children like Gig could open up a can of worms. Don't you want the past buried?"

"You can only bury it for awhile, Mom. Someday Gig will have to know that his dad isn't dead and isn't far."

"He must be far now. His cousin May told me that he's in England. She can tell by the sound of his letters, even though the place names are all scratched out by the army. See! Secrets again! Gen, secrets can be good."

"Do you ever run into Randy's parents, Mom?"

"Once in awhile I see his mother at the store but she's a stranger to me, Gen. I honestly believe she and her husband know nothing about you...and Gig."

"Guys can keep that secret pretty well. Unfortunately, my waist couldn't."

"Do we have enough lard?"

"Thank God for you and Dad and the Sisters at St. Scholastica. They were a home away from home and made sure I learned something from the mistake. They were even supportive when I told them that I wouldn't give the baby up for adoption."

"Hmmm. I hope those aren't mouse droppings."

"You could have booted me out," Gen said, seating herself on a kitchen chair.

"Nonsense. One mistake was enough. And enough said, girl. Let's catch the rest of the parlor show." Saying that, she squeezed her daughter's hand and led her into the living room.

A few days later, the family drove to Paul's house to see if he had pumpkin seed for a project in science Sister Heribert had started for Gig and his school companions. Three grades shared one room so there would be several cans of dirt on the window sills containing several kinds of seeds.

"Yah, I got some," Paul said matter of factly, "if I can find it right now. You can sure tell Sister comes from a farm family. It's a good way to learn though, isn't it, boy?" Gig's uncle winked at him. "Seeds are as interesting as, uh, heck." His eyes caught his sister's accidentally and both of them then looked in different directions.

The grandfather was checking the plowed fields and snooping around the out buildings as the former planter would. He usually found no fault with Paul's farming. After all, hadn't Paul been his best pupil when it came to the farm? His other children appreciated the farm but not as much as Paul and their interests took them in different directions.

Gen's life had been rearranged by her pregnancy and the Benedictine Sisters had put her to work in their hospital kitchen in Pine Bluff while she waited for her child. Since she was still a teenager, the Sisters educated her and gave her a diploma from their academy. All of the Sisters had been mothers to her, except, of course, Mary and Ida, who kept sisterly eyes on her, all to the great comfort of their parents back in Missouri.

Occasionally, Gen mused that, were she not responsible for Gig, she would have joined her sisters in the convent. But, with the wisdom she had gained through fear, regret, and the joy of childbirth, she concluded that the vocation of mothering was just as holy and she put herself to the task.

Gig had gone with his cousin Theresa to get a Folger's Coffee can full of dirt. Theresa made him sprinkle some cow manure in it to improve its quality. She knew all about this project and, as a matter of fact, she was one of Sister's favorites others said.

As Paul and his sister watched from the back porch, they laughed as their dad lectured his grandchildren about soil. Their mother and Felicia joined them. " He should have been a professor," Rose said. "Or an auctioneer."

"I found that pumpkin seed," Paul shouted at the trio by the barn.

"Just a minute," the elder Bauer called back. He never let an interruption terminate a lecture. His wife was right about his tendency to teach. He took every opportunity to do so and even Rose felt that it was such a special quality that it passed to their children giving then all characteristic sense and sensitivity. There were occasional lapses but they seemed to increase the wisdom in the long run. That was their father's gift. Their mother's gift was the living of a rhythm of life that included the garden, her housework, her charity, and her religion.

As they were about to head for the house, Gig pointed to the small field behind the barn.

"Why are all those big slabs of rock in that part of the farm, Grandpa?"

"They've always been there. That field was like that when your grandma inherited the farm from Mr. Henry Huber, your great-grandpa. He must have dragged them there or somebody before him. That's a good question. I've always wondered myself. The rest of the land isn't rocky. Maybe they wanted to keep the stones handy for future use, say if a foundation got weak or caved." Gig's grandfather was not being evasive. In fact, he had the boy's mind aglow with imagination.

" Maybe they were standing rocks and those German boys crouched behind them to shoot at the bushwhackers."

"So you didn't forget about that?" noted his grand-father.

"Forget? Don't you think that's important, Grandpa?"

"Well...take my advice, Gig. Don't talk about the bushwhackers to your grandma. It upsets her."

"Why?" both of the children asked.

"Can't say," was the old man's response. "Let's get that pumpkin seed now."

"How many seeds you want, Farmer Gig?" his uncle asked when they were on the porch.

"Can I have two?"

" Take three. Plant three. A seed might be dead and you won't know it 'til you can't grow it." The last remark was about the extent of his uncle's wittiness. "Take your finger and poke three nesting holes. Halfway down in the can. Good."

The young farmer dropped a pumpkin seed into each hole and his nephew covered them well with dirt. "Now," his uncle continued," you should give them drops of water everyday. But not too much."

"Wait a minute!" Grandma interjected. "I've got just the thing and she extracted a small bottle of Lourdes Water from her purse. Then she dribbled some of the holy water on the soil. "Bless us, O Lord, and these Thy gifts." Then quick as a flash, she struck each of those present with at least one drop of the water in an eye, on a nose, or in an ear.

"You're too extravagant with that water, Grandma," her husband warned. "Don't forget that the French can't ship it to us for awhile."

"When I run out, so will the Nazis!" she snapped back with a great smile.

Then for about two hours, the family remained in the cheery farm house enjoying Sunday. Since it was Lent, the meal tasted tastier because the adults were fasting during the rest of the week from excessive food and abstaining from meat dishes. Father Luke said that the Church's discipline supported the war effort. He was secretly proud that he had no parishoners who were overweight.

About four o'clock the group from Wallenhorst headed for the car parked near the barn. For a few minutes, Gig prowled around the rocks in the small field he had investigated earlier with his grandfather.

"Out of the boneyard!" Grandma Bauer called.

Gig was sure she meant to say barnyard but it sounded so much like boneyard.

"And don't forget your pumpkin patch!" his mother said.

The car rolled out of the yard past the barn with figures in and out of it waving goodbye.

"Grandpa," Gig asked, " could you say that the rocky field behind the barn is fallow?"

"I suppose so, " was the driver's reply.

"I think it's going to rain again," his wife interrupted.

"My uncle has a fallow field. Fallow. F-a-l-l-o-w. Fallow." the boy chanted.

"Good!" the driver exclaimed.

As the car headed back to town, Gen leaned against the back seat and took herself into her deeper thoughts. "Fallow," she thought to herself. "F-a-l-l-o-w. Gen is a fallow field, a fallow woman." She thought about her status as a single woman. She was pleased with her decision not to hide Gig but, in a small town, she was a ready mystery. Most wanted to assume that she had become widowed while she was in Pine Bluff but saw little of widowhood in her. She was a mystery to herself as well. She closed her eyes and said to some guardian spirit,"Show the path."

Gig watched his mother for a few minutes and, once again, said to himself, "My mother is the prettiest woman in town. She is as pretty as the picture of the Blessed Mother in Grandma's bedroom.

"Gen, did you remember to put Easter Egg dye on the shopping list?"

"Ummhmm," her daughter replied.

"Grandpa, is an egg fallow?"

"I have to think about that," the driver answered. "Don't you want to work with some other words?"

"I do believe the boy has stumped you, Professor, " Rose Bauer commented.

"Never!" her husband asserted.

Purple clouds hung over the country as the aging car left little clouds of dust behind it and neared Wallenhorst. The season of Lent deepened. Easter was not far away.

THE LAST STORYTELLER

It was quietly agreed that the four of them would visit the Bells. Gig's grandmother did not protest but she was eager to get done with it. Gig was told that they were paying respects to the family because a son had been killed in the war. The man was buried " where he fell" according to Mr. Bauer. Gig pictured a battlefield which impressed him like the picture of Gettysburg he had seen in a library book.

In the house, other people from Wallenhorst were shaking hands with Mr. and Mrs. Bell, who were standing beside a photograph of a handsome young soldier. Gig didn't remember ever seeing the soldier around town but he heard that the Bells were Methodists and probably did not mix much with Catholics. His grandfather had said that differences should be laid aside when it came to grief. His mother had not said much since the word arrived that Randy Bell had been killed in action.

Mrs. Bell thanked Mrs. Bauer for the chocolate meringue pie she brought, as she handed it to one of the Methodist ladies who had come to help her. The people of Wallenhorst were not given to much emotional displays but these two women understood the cost of motherhood. When Mrs. Bell saw Gen, she smiled. "Gen, I appreciate your coming too. Randy had such a crush on you. But you must remember how silly he was in high school. Just like a butterfly."

Randy's mother did not notice Gig and her husband was deep in conversation with their pastor.

Gen gave the Mrs. Bell a smile and then moved to a younger woman seated next to a little girl.

Gen spoke first. "Mrs. Bell?"

"Yes?" the young widow replied.

"I'm Gen. I was in high school with your husband."

"Then you knew him well, I suppose," the sad voice responded.

"I believe he would say so." Gen asked her guardian angel to put the right words in her mouth for the visit to the Bells.

"Didn't I just hear someone say that you're a widow too? Is this your little boy?"

"Yes," Gen said, giving just one answer for the two questions.

"You can understand how I feel then. This is Randy's little girl, Missy."

"And this is my little boy, Gig," Gen echoed.

"I feel sorry for the children..." Randy's widow started, but then began to cry.

Gen knelt down beside her and held her lightly. Gig stared at the confused little girl, who was about three or four. He didn't know what to say to her.

Mrs. Bauer was not given to tears but when she saw her daughter's compassion and the children standing by their mothers, her eyes filled rapidly with sorrow and pride. She took her grandson's hand and led him to the front porch to join her husband, who was discussing the war with some of his old friends.

It was her custom each night to sprinkle her household with holy water and that night, after the males had gone to bed, Rose spoke to Gen:

"Gen, you know that I am proud of Phil and her family. I'm nuts about my sons. And I am happy to have two daughters in the convent. But none of them could hold a candle to you today. When I saw what you did for that poor girl and how much love you wrapped around her,

I thought I would die with pride. Tonight I could die as a fulfilled mother."

Gen was almost unconscious with surprise. Her mother never spoke like that! She started to walk toward her.

Her mother stepped into the pantry. "Where did you put the Easter dye?"

Easter Sunday was a house full. The aromatic ham presided over all. Everyone who passed it before and after the grand meal picked at it, as though it was a newly di-covered treat. Much of the food joined to the ham was a product of planting, harvesting, and canning by the family.

Mr. Bauer's homemade wine and beer tickled the adults who let the children run wild in and out of the house. The weather was proper in its celebration of the Resurrection, winter having given way to spring.

Richard and his mother came from Kansas City and were able to stay the week afterwards. Catholic schools dismissed their students in observation of the Great Feast of the Resurrection. Richard and Gig were going to join the men of the family for a night of fishing at Goose Lake, which was actually back water from Clear Creek running through the Bauer farm.

Many old fish swam there and the men in Gig's family considered them their personal prey. Occasional camping at Goose Lake also gave the men the opportunity to introduce the boys to the male traditions. So, Grandpa would have Gig and Richard as his charges on Easter Sunday night.

"If they get tired, put them on the car seats," Grandma bossed. "Don't let them lie out in the damp."

"When the Chevie reached the farm and passed the barn, Gig told Richard that they were passing the fallow field.

"What's that?" his cousin asked.

"I'll tell you more later."

"Can't you talk in front of me, Gig?" his grandfather questioned.

"You don't seem to know much about it, Grandpa."

"That's what you think. First of all...There's your cousins, already starting the fire."

The fallow field was forgotten and the three joined the gathering cousins who were arranging tackle, water jugs, and boxes of left-over Easter food. The grandfather had his two squires add their equipment to the gear around the fire. They helped him fashion a rough lean-to with some fallen branches, an old tarp, against a venerable walnut tree. The scene was an annual ritual and the first time Richard and Gig were permitted to stay overnight. They both felt like young braves in a hunting party.

Uncle Paul had brought the boat out of storage and hauled it to the lake with his tractor and trailer. While there was sunlight, the men got it into the water so that they could check it for any leaks. After a half hour in the water, the elders thought the boat sea worthy and placed what the first crew would need aboard. Grandpa and his charges went first. He wanted to be able to see them and to be able to teach them about fishing. He also knew they would get tired too soon to plan on any night fishing with them.

They glided out to the center and the boys watched their hero man the oars with perfect rhythm. They felt safe and confident that their grandsire would pull in a great catch. And, sure enough, he brought in a large catfish, which would feed his clan that night, after a fry in a great black skillet. Satisfied with his good fortune, the elder brought the boat to the little dock and let the boys run the path with the fish while he secured the craft.

It was almost dusk and a large fire was going. The men were drinking beer and eating ham sandwiches. Their grandfather had the boys put the catfish in a tub of lake water until there would be sufficient fish to gut and fillet. Then he took a cold beer And cheered on the other grandsons who headed for the boat. "Get some perch, boys!"

About that time an antique truck pulled into the lane by the lake and Martin Meyer ambled up to the fire. Martin was well over eighty and was one of the treasures of the county because he knew more stories and more families than anyone else. His visits were a treat in any house. He played the fiddle. He still danced at weddings! He could always be called upon for an eloquent toast at any kind of banquet including funerals. He was also a reliable historian, though he wrote nothing down. He had his Missouri twang but there was a bit of German in it, especially obvious when he spoke word beginning with V—making it a W and vice versa. "He vas a wery good man" was one of his frequent tributes.

Since he was related to this gathering by blood, his presence was even more delightful. Paul Bauer hauled an old lawn chair off his trailer for him and he sat in it like a noble visitor, his hands gripping the ends of each arm rest. Everyone waited on him with food, drink, and questions about his health and well-being. The fire even seemed to greet him and lit his face with a radiant glow. In turn, he greeted each by name, including the youngest of the lot. He asked about the women, including the two in the convent. He smacked his lips with gratitude as he guzzled his beer and pulled at his ham sandwich. The older men knew that he was getting oiled for stories.

Someone mentioned something about a mean boar and that got Martin to start: "Do you all remember Wernon Schneider? He had more trouble vith pigs! And no vonder. You did not know his fader. Dot poor man!"

As in a ritual, Paul asked," What was wrong with him?"

"His own pigs ate him." Martin Meyer said abruptly.

Richard and his cousin looked at each other with wide eyes. The had spent time in the pig pen helping their uncle. Both of them started to think about man-eating pigs.

Martin Meyer chewed at his ham sandwich and sucked at his teeth for punctuation marks.

"Yah...Yah... He must have tripped and hit his head." He looked at the saucer eyes of the children. He sucked his teeth again and smacked his lips.

"When?" Richard gasped.

"Must've been around the turn, before the var, de uder var, 'cause Wernon vas just a boy like dese. He found vat vas left of his fader. Ach! Tink of dot."

"Did they keep those pigs?" Emil Bauer asked.

"Vell, de ol' lady she sold dem right then. Didn't vant to eat her ol' man vith de ham."

Gig and Richard nearly retched, thinking about the ham they just ate.

After a few more beers, Martin Meyer was talking about all the old folks and passing on what he had heard about their German ancestors. The fire would flare occasionally as though it was licking up his stories too.

Finally, Gig took his turn with a question to the storyteller. He came right to the point.

"Who's buried in the fallow field behind the old barn over there?" He pointed in the direction of the Bauer farmyard.

"Dem bushvhackers, of course," the old man declared. "Dey got our dander up!"

"Our?" Gig gasped. " Were YOU there?"

"No, but who ve is is who our faders vere. So ve vas there too. All you boys here!"

"What happened there?" the others chimed in.

Martin Meyer related how their relatives, new to the United States, were constantly harassed by men who took advantage of them. And then, one day, some bushwhackers came to rob this very farm and the young men shot them dead."

He was interrupted by shouts coming closer from the lake and then by the brothers stepping up to the firelight with a catch of perch. It was time to fry and all except Gig and Richard forgot about the bushwhackers. A short while later, they were lying and talking, each on a car seat. Archaeology appealed to both of them and they talked of digging up the "boneyard" as Gig now called it. Martin Meyer had let a cat out of the bag. A cat with huge eyes, two flaming fires, glaring at two excited boys.

THE BONEYARD

Richard and Gig talked for a while. Gig recalled how he thought Grandma called the fallow field "boneyard." "There's something to that. A clue!" he said dramatically to his cousin.

Richard added his two cents. "Did you notice how Martin Meyer didn't even have to stop and think about the dead guys?"

Grandpa came near the car and heard Richard's part of the conversation. "You guys aren't going to give up on that story, are you? Now you know, or you should know, that Martin Meyer is a great storyteller but he dresses up his stories quite a bit."

Gig asked his grandfather if he doubted Martin Meyer's word.

"Beer can make a colorful story out of a bit of truth," said the elder.

"Have you heard the same story before?" Richard asked.

"Well...yes."

"Has it changed much?"

"Well...no."

Gig interrupted both of them. "I believe it and I want to prove it!"

"How?" said Richard.

"Digging" was the reply.

"Do you think your uncle will let you dig up his field?" the elder challenged.

"It's just a fallow field. Unsown. Untilled." Gig retorted.

"Smarty pants!" Grandpa laughed. Then he let Richard in on the vocabulary lesson.

Martin Meyer wandered over by the car. The two boys shot up from the car seats, casting off any drowsiness.

"Mister Meyer, can you tell us more about the bushwhackers?" Richard asked.

"Yah. Yah. But not tonight. Its time I vas in bed. Yah. But some other time."

"How many were there, Martin Meyer?" Gig demanded, wanting detail.

"Three. For sure. Vell, good night. Don't let the bedbugs bite." Martin Meyer headed for his old truck, grinded the ignition, and puttered off to his house on the other side of Clear Creek.

"You two lie down and get some sleep. I don't want the wrath of three women bushwhacking me."

The boys each wrapped themselves in their jackets and bade their hero goodnight at the same time he wished them a good night. When their grandfather walked away,

Gig said," There are two spades in the barn." A cat spirit sat by him and peered through the dark, through the trees, past the fields, and to the barnyard. By then the cousins were joined in sleep.

In the morning about 6:30, the men woke up the boys who had managed to sleep well in the comfort of the car. The men had a mess of fish, having spent most of the night in serious work, mostly silent, sometimes excited because of competition. Now the plan was to meet the women at Paul's house after the men had napped so that lunch could start at noon. So about 7:00, all of the fishing party slipped into the house to wash and then to nap until the ladies arrived.

Gig and Richard each had a biscuit and jelly with a glass of cold milk and watched furtively while the rest found places to nap on couches, spare beds, or pallets on the floor of the living room. Then, the boys stole from the kitchen, out of the house, to the barn and found the spades. In just a few more minutes, as their relatives slept, they stood at the edge of the fallow field. Their aunt Felicia was the only relative stirring but because she was so preoccupied with food preparation, she did not notice her two nephews standing in the field near the barn.

"Where shall we start?"

"I've been thinking," Gig murmured, while still think- ing," that stone there might have been put on the grave to keep dogs from digging." It was a long flat stone from the creek bed. Oblong. It was probably about four feet in length and no more than four inches thick. It lay on the ground like a flag stone. Using the handles of their spades like crowbars, the boys lifted one side of the stone and then flipped it over. From under it appeared the usual gray roly-poly beetles which loved dark, moist places.

"I just had a great idea, Richard. We can say we're digging for fishing worms if anyone asks." Gig grinned. Then he pierced the ground with his spade, which set Richard into motion.

They dug surely but slowly. The gulps of dirt on their spades were a lot to lift. A pile of dirt opposite the over-turned stone rose steadily. Richard went and found an old bucket, pitched in some clods, and picked out some worms for the sake of explanation if need be.

They had dug for about 45 minutes when Richard struck the earth with a soft promising thud of discovery. Both boys heard the mysterious sound and paused simul-taneously. Then they spaded more cautiously and within minutes had uncovered a rotted wrap of leather and within it a bone!

"Don't move it! Don't move it!" Gig whispered loudly to his cousin. " Dig around it 'til we get the whole skeleton." So they dug around the bone which became a shaft of bone but no more. No other bones were in the hold except the shaft and its extension which became a knee, a lower leg, and a foot complete with tiny bones packed in the dirt.

Gig ran to the house to see if anyone was noticing. He heard his aunt moving around softly so as not to disturb the sleepers. He figured it was close to 9:00. He then ran inside the barn and found a gunny sack and returned to the hole to help Richard lift the discovery out of the hole.

"Gosh," Richard exclaimed," it must be a yard long!"

"A man's leg, for sure," his cousin proclaimed like Sherlock. "Keep some of the dirt packed around it to hold it together." Now Gig was acting like a scientist as well as a detective. They propped open the mouth of the sack and the both of them slid the bones into it. Carefully, they rolled the burlap around it. But then Richard had an idea. "Find a board to put in the bag with the bones like a splint. Nothing will break then."

"Good idea!" Gig fetched a short board from the wood shed and placed it in the bag with the bones tied to it at various strategic points. They took the leg to their grandfather's car and stowed it in the trunk over and under some old newspapers their elder kept there for a variety of uses. When they slammed the trunk, their aunt came out of the back door to see what they were doing.

Gig was quick to conceal the purpose of their dirt and digging. "Want to see some juicy worms, Aunt Felicia?" He ran behind the barn and brought out to the car the bucket of dirt.

"That's O.K.," their aunt said, uninterested in fishing worms. "You'd better get cleaned up before long. It's 9:30

now and your mothers will be here soon." The boys nodded and she returned to the kitchen, careful not to let the screen door slam.

The youngsters returned to the barnyard and filled up the hole rapidly, occasionally extracting a worm for the bucket. Then they flipped the stone over the disturbed earth to conceal their work. Some evidence of digging still remained but, having active imaginations and ideas from war movies, they strewed straw and powdered manure over the loose dirt and even over the stone. "Now let's get cleaned up," Gig moved and they got into the house just as a car pulled into the driveway full of women who would surely wake the men.

As they dirtied the bathroom sink, the boys decided to remove the leg from the trunk of the car shortly after returning to Wallenhorst. "I'll take it to the attic when Grandpa goes to bed. But you'll have to distract the others, Richard."

"No problem. Hey, look at this sink! We'd better clear up this mess. We don't need any investigations. Richard mopped up the sink with a navy blue towel, then pitched it into the bathtub.

"Did they behave?" Phil inquired.

"Good as gold!" their Aunt Felicia declared.

The Easter Monday meal was another celebration with the addition of fried fresh fish. Felicia wanted her Easter meal to exceed her mother-in-law's in bulk and beauty although she would never have admitted to that desire. Eggs! She had rainbow eggs. Chocolate eggs. Decorated eggs. Baskets of eggs all over the place! There was sausage, ham, fried chicken, and the fish of course. Mountains of mashed potatoes! Green beans. Pinto beans. The kitchen was full of empty Mason Jars which had been filled by Felicia and Theresa during the previous summer. Her mother-in-law scanned the scene thoroughly.

And now Felicia's children were acting as waiters and a waitress, bringing food and drink to their elders and their cousins. Gen and Phil offered the services of their sons but Paul and Felicia were so taken with the two's good behavior, they would not have it said that they worked them at Easter. Once Theresa stuck out her tongue at Gig when he said he wanted more cider. Only he saw it and he returned the gesture.

Joseph Schuster appeared in the middle of dessert and shyly sat next to Gen. Phil winked at her sister. "How was Easter at your place, Joe?" Grandpa asked him.

"Noise and feed. Noise and feed."

"I hear Father Gabriel came from the Abbey," Grandma remarked.

"No, Mrs. Bauer, he's coming this week though. He doesn't have to teach and he's going to give Father Boniface a rest. Father Boniface will probably drive to Maryville to see his cousin."

"I take it your brother will stay in the rectory," Grandma asserted. She liked to know that everything was in order.

45

"Yah. It's more room for him."

"Your mother must be glad he's around," Grandma continued.

"Well, yah, but he's not special, if you know what I mean." He smiled at Gen.

"Good," Grandma declared," we can't have favorites."

Gen smiled at Joe. For all his plainness, he was dear to her. His expression said that he had a favorite. He could not have tolerated more noise, were not Gen at the gathering. He barely noticed the meringue on his lemon pie as he kept his eyes on her.

"Don't you kids want to go outside?" Grandpa questioned and, in a wink, the youth disappeared. Silas and Martin took a tractor ride to the Twenter farm about a mile away. Philip went upstairs to listen to war reports and Theresa, pocketing several chocolate eggs wrapped in foil, went to her room to wade through the movie magazines Aunt Phil had brought from Kansas City. Their cousins generally liked Gig and Richard but the little bit of difference in their lives and in their ages drew a thin curtain between them. Silas, for instance, thought Gig was too much of a bookworm and Richard too much like Gig.

The pair did not care. They walked to their grand-father's car and leaned against the door of the trunk. "Richard, have you thought about the fact that there was not a whole skeleton?"

"I don't want to think why. Do you think the Hubers hacked the robbers to pieces?"

Both boys seemed embarrassed by Richard's question because they were, after all, close relatives to the Hubers.

NIGHTMARES

After sleeping on car seats, after digging and refilling a rather large hole, and after the horrible thrill of discovering the leg, the cousins were primed for a deep sleep that Monday.

Once bathed, then sprinkled with holy water by their grandmother, Richard and Gig both climbed into the large featherbed and wished each other a good night.

Gig remarked, " Did you ever wonder why people say 'Good Night'? Is sleeping anything but good?"

"Maybe you want the other person not to have nightmares," his cousin sighed sleepily.

He was fading, getting closer to the "other world." "Do YOU ever have nightmares?" Gig continued. But he received no response.

Richard was peeping through a knot hole in the side of a large shed. His eye was pressed hard because most of what he saw was shadows. He heard voices and they were clearer than the shadows. They were speaking with German accents. One of the voices sounded like Martin Meyer or did it? He blinked and tried to stare harder. But

Richard never seemed to get the investigation to focus. Bits of the conversation didn't make sense.

"Who else vould know about dem?" a strong voice asked. "They are no more than drek.

Dirt!"

"That's right," a younger voice said. "They had no right to be in our yard." That voice like the other was angry.

Richard blinked and blinked. He strained to know the voices. "What yard?" he thought.

Then he felt his feet getting cold. "Was it the bone-yard?" he wondered.

"Vhat did you do vith their horses, Clement?"

"They are in the far barn. I stripped the gear and gave them something to eat after Henry rubbed them down."

"He shouldn't be around those horses. They're as unpredictable as their riders. A bad lot—all of them!" the older voice said.

Richard couldn't figure out the owners of anything, voices or horses. It agitated him. Then he put his ear on the knot hole but, strange, he couldn't hear anything. While he was bent, he felt something brush against him. He was found! But by whom? Certainly by strangers!

The thing, whatever, whoever, it was began to bump against him and pulled at his jacket. Richard froze. Then he saw an eye coming into his view. A large wild eye! It seemed to be looking for something, someone. The pupil of it went up; it went down; it went to the right; to the left. Looking. Looking. It ran into him and Richard perceived it to be a horse. Then not one horse, but two. No! Three!

The three animals pawed at him, as though they were demanding that he surrender to them whatever they were looking for. The voices in the shed had grown much dimmer. The horses looked down into Richard's heart. One of them said to him," Where is my master? Where have you taken him?" Richard could not speak. The horses bumped him again and again with their muzzles.

Then he saw a man coming through the blackness. He had a crutch because he had only one leg. He did not know anyone with one leg. He tried to wrap himself up with shadows. "Where are the horses?" the approaching voice asked. "Are they worth it? Will I have to kill them too?" Richard flattened himself against the shed. He wished Gig was with him. Or did he wish that Richard was with him? "Who am I?" the boy thought.

The voice was on top of him. "Where are my horses?" The voice was a trio of voices.

Bloodshot eyes appeared like a constellation of stars but they were eyes of horses and men. Indistinguishable. The boy held his breath. He knew that he was about to faint. And just as he did, a trap door opened and his body floated like a feather down and down into a pile of cotton.

There he lay unconscious.

Gig went looking for his cousin. He was on a twisting road that wound into the country. He saw trees and fields that he recognized. He enjoyed the search at first because he knew he would find his best friend, his first cousin. He enjoyed the warmth on his face and tried to ignore the cold breeze on his back. But it finally irritated him so much that he turned to face its source.

What he saw astounded him. There were three horses breathing on him but not with the warm breath of living horses. These horses were barely more than skeletons. Neglected and starved, the horses were at once weak and wild. Gig stared at their solemn eyes before he noted that each of them had a rider. One man had no face. One was a young soldier in uniform but barefoot. One was a teenage boy with a large grin.

Somehow the man with no face spoke," Son, can you tell us where to find the Huber place?"

Before Gig could respond, the soldier said to the first voice," Do you know Gen Huber?"

Then the boy on the horse said," She's a LOT of fun!"

"Son?" the first voice questioned Gig.

"I used to know," Gig said," but I don't think I know anymore. If we can find my cousin, he could help us."

The trio of horses bearing the men swayed, creating more of a cold breeze.

Gig thought he heard cicadas in the trees overhead. They sawed softly. He looked up and then when his eyes returned to the road there was nothing of horses and riders except only a great deal of droppings. The figures had not frightened Gig but he became agitated when he realized that so much time had elapsed and he still could not find Richard. The cicadas continued their noise and the shadows of the trees crept entirely across his path.

He started down the road again but he fell. No wonder. He only had one leg!

"Only one leg?" he asked himself with more curiosity than discomfort. Then he realized what he was asking. "Only one leg! Only one leg!" he screamed. Someone grabbed him! He screamed again! He heard a whisper say," Quiet, Gig! You'll give us away!" It was Richard! He had found him. They had found each other. Gig was so glad about that, that he collapsed in the road and relaxed in the shade of the trees.

When the sun evaporated the shadows, Gig opened one eye and saw his cousin sleeping beside him.

"Hey, Richard!"

Richard rolled on his side and squinted in the direction of his alter ego. Then he hissed,"

You almost gave us away last night, screaming about the leg."

"What are you talking about?"

"Gig, you were talking in your sleep about the one leg. Loud too!"

"I remember some kind of dream about some weird guys on horses and I was afraid of being a cripple, I think."

"You mean you don't remember screaming?"

"Nah. Do you always remember your dreams?"

"Sorry, Gig, but I don't dream."

Later, while they were at the kitchen table, they continued a kind of conversation.

"Hmmm, more family secrets," Gig mumbled. His grandma arched an eyebrow.

"I was just wondering," Richard said dreamily. The name Clement is in my head."

"Did Martin Meyer talk about him the other night?" Gig asked his cousin.

"Dunno. Don't remember."

"I'll tell you boys one thing," their grandmother declared," Between Martin Meyer and Virgil Kempchen, you boys are goin' to go crazy. They have more bats in their belfries than the towers of Capistrano."

Both boys laughed. "Capistrano has swallows," Richard told her.

"It used to," their grandma retorted. "But folks out there listened to too many stories and the bats took over." As she spoke, her husband entered the kitchen.

"Speaking of bats," he said," would you boys like to go to the Knights of Columbus game with the Lions' Club at 5:00? It's the warm-up game for the year. Your mothers are taking their mother shopping. And you wouldn't enjoy that cackling I know."

"I'd better shake a leg!" Rose said as she rose.

Then Gig remembered that the leg was still in his grandfather's car under the newspapers in the trunk.

Before she left the room, Richard asked his grand-mother if she ever knew anyone with the name Clement.

"I know a few men in the parish with that name on their baptismal records but none of them go by it. They go by Clem."

"I heard it somewhere and it stuck in my mind for some reason," her grandson continued.

"I had an Uncle Clement but I never met him. He was your great-grandfather Huber's elder brother but he died as a young man. Hadn't even made it to marriage. That's why I got the farm. Because Dad was the only remaining boy."

"Did he live on the farm with somebody named Henry?"

"Well, Lord, yes! My dad's name was Henry. Surely you knew that!

"Yeah, I guess I did."

Gig then moved into the conversation. "What killed Clement?"

"Whatever do you mean by that?" Rose demanded.

"Well, he died young. Was it war? Or bushwhackers?"

"No," she replied. "Isn't that funny though. I only know he was sick but I don't know what killed him. Dad never talked about him much. Well, I gotta go."

"I gotta go too." Gig winked at Richard on his way to the trunk of his grandfather's car.

A BAD CONFESSION

As the last of May drew near, Sister Heribert urged her students to get themselves in spiritual shape for the summer. Among other duties, she reminded them to receive the sacraments of penance and holy communion regularly. Parents were very grateful to the young nun because she made their job easier. The children were devoted to the attractive and energetic teacher and they were not slow to follow her directions and suggestions. They felt as though she loved them as much as their parents and made efforts never to offend her.

At the beginning of the summer vacation, Sister Heribert would travel back to the priory, which was in Arkansas, to rejoin all the Sisters. There she would study and work and pray with two hundred women like her, including Gig's aunts, Sister Hildegard and Sister Mechtild. In fact, Sister Heribert and Sister Hildegard were the same age. Sister Heribert had already promised that she would take a package to Gig's aunts from his grandparents and others who wanted to fill the portable box. In it would be handkerchiefs, soap, candy, toothbrushes, toothpaste, black shoe laces, and pencils. The family knew that their "special two" would share the articles with the rest of the Sisters but that made the packing even more delightful.

Rose packed another box for the four Sisters stationed in Wallenhorst, which was full of food and drink for their long train ride. This had been an accepted tradition for years and the Sisters missioned in Wallenhorst called Mrs. Bauer "Mother Rose." Other families in the parish provided car rides, occasional jars and cans of food, linen, and what have you but "Mother Rose" provided the train treats and even carried it on board before she hugged all the Sisters goodbye.

Gig was not the recipient of easy treatment because of the Sisters' attachment to his family. He was, in fact, more careful of his behavior because of the "conspiracy of women" as Grandpa called the conditions surrounding himself and Gig. Neither was Gig unique because many of the students had aunts, cousins, and even sisters at the same convent in Arkansas. He could already figure out which of his classmates would eventually enter the Benedictine community and join the "conspiracy of women."

When word came that the Sisters were leaving Wallenhorst on the first Monday in June, a procession of well-wishers conveyed them to the depot even though the train departed at 6:30 A.M. sharp. Gig was roused to help carry the box of food and to say goodbye to Sister Heribert and the other three Sisters who were all like children eager for the excitement. No talk of school or parish but only messages being memorized for Sisters in Arkansas. Gig escaped the passenger car before his mother and grandmother and joined his grandfather on the platform.

"Noisy even at 6:00 A.M., no matter if nun or non-nun. That's women for you," Mr. Bauer informed his grandson. About then, the conductor cleared the car of all except the passengers and, a few minutes later, a shrill whistle preceded the lively waving from the windows and to the windows.

"Hurry up, Gig," his mother cried at the dozy boy parked on a bench next to his grandpa. "You've got to serve the 7:00 mass!" And then Gig was off on foot to join Father Boniface at St. Hilda's. Thus he began and continued his turn as an acolyte that week, moving through the mass ritual like a dancer and returning Latin prayers for Latin prayers during the course of the liturgy. "Ad Deum qui laetificat juventutem meum..."

Father Boniface asked if the Sisters departed without difficulty.

"Yes, Father."

He also asked if his Benedictine aunts would visit home soon.

"No, Father."

Then he asked if there would be summer visitors in Wallenhorst to see the Bauers.

"Yes, Father. My cousin Richard is coming from Kansas City next Sunday, Father."

"That 's nice. Behave yourselves and help your grandparents this summer. Make their lives easier."

"Yes, Father." Gig was glad that manners gave him words to say to the priest.

After mass, Father Boniface gave the boy a stick of gum and after he had straightened out the sacristy, Gig headed home for a hot breakfast. While they were eating, Grandpa was looking at a LIFE magazine and reading to everyone about a bombardment which had plowed through a German cemetery.

"Ach!" Rose clucked. "War! Why? Why do the dead have to get involved?"

Gen shook her head. "Imagine! Desecrating graves! Surely it wasn't intentional!"

"That's what bad about wars," Rose declared after sipping her coffee. "Chaos takes over."

"Two words!" Gig cried.

Bemused, his grandfather asked," What's that all about?"

"Sister Heribert said to learn one unfamiliar word every day during the summer."

"What words then?" Gen inquired.

"Dezgrate and K-Oats," her son replied.

"Repeat after me," his mother instructed. "De-se-crate. Cha-os."

"What do they mean?"

"The first word means messing around with a sacred or holy item. In other words, a graveyard should never be disturbed for the sake of the souls whose bones are there. That's why we bless graves. Now, chaos," Gen continued," means disorder and confusion—like your room. Nothing in its proper place."

Gig paid little attention to the second definition because he was thinking about the first. "Disturbing bones is unholy," he said to himself. Now his food didn't have any taste.

After breakfast, Gig went to his grandmother's garden and pulled weeds while the ground was still damp with dew. "Weeds are like lesser sins," Rose told him once. "Better get rid of them before they root and get bigger." Gig couldn't help but think of sin that morning, especially the sin of "dezgration." The thought of sin made his weed extractions rapid but thorough. (Rose always had great comparisons.)

When he came into the house for a drink of water, his grandfather asked him if he wanted to go the sale barn. The sale barn gave Emil Bauer an opportunity to spend time with his cronies and sometimes he made contacts for butchering. Local folk would often buy cattle or hogs and ask Emil to kill them and butcher them because he was so good at it. In fact, Gig and his cousins had their first anatomy lessons with their grandfather, as they took turns helping him with butchering. Blood and guts did not bother them because Emil had explained the cycle of life to them. They knew very well that nourishment required preparation and that butchering was part of it.

Gig went with his grandpa to the sale barn. In fact they spent a great deal of time together on projects devised by Emil...and Rose...and Gen. Each day that week started with serving mass and then involved Gig in multiple projects and pleasures, such as a farm town provided. That first week in June sped and Saturday came soon. And on Saturday afternoon, Gig joined the line of parishoners who went to confession at St. Hilda's.

As he knelt in the church and read the examination of conscience in his missal, he could find no sin called "dezgration." He went through the list of sins twice. "Well," he said to himself," if it's not on the list, it must not be a sin." So, he went into the confessional with a small list of small sins, venial sins, as Sister Heribert called them. The dezgration nagged him as he told his sins to Father Boniface, who was behind a curtained window, and Gig remembered that Sister told the kids that if they had questions or doubts they should mention them to the priest after stating their sins. Gig didn't want to ask about dezgration because it sounded so bad.

"Father Boniface sounds like he's in a hurry," Gig tried to tell himself and he let the priest conclude the ritual without stating his doubt.

When Gig returned to a pew to say his penance, he looked at the tabernacle and started to recite the penance-prayers automatically, then an uneasy feeling clamped his heart and he thought to himself that he had just made a BAD confession. That was worse than dezgration. He sweated a little. He could not pray. And then his mother tugged at his sleeve to leave with the family. As they walked home together, Gig suddenly mentioned that he needed to get something from church and ran back to the building. "I'll see you at home," he shouted over his shoulder.

Inside the church, he waited until anyone, who had seen him enter the confessional earlier, had left the church. Then he slipped into the short line of new arrivals. When his turn came, he knelt inside the dark compartment, perspiring again, waiting for the sliding door to open the little window where priest and penitent conversed. When the door opened, Gig spoke rapidly. "Blessme Father for I have sinned. My last confession was ten minutes ago. These are my sins."

He reiterated his list of venial sins and then he said," I made a bad confession. I did not ask you a question."

There was a bit of silence. Gig thought maybe he heard a chuckle but he could not imagine a priest laughing over such a serious matter. Then, Father Boniface asked," What was the question?"

"Is dezgration a mortal or venial sin?"

"Is what?"

"Dezgration."

"What is dezgration."

"Messing with bones."

"Gig, what is wrong with you?

"Gasp!" The boy was shocked. Confession is always secret and the priest knew his identity!

"What is wrong with you, Boy?"

"I made a bad confession because I didn't ask a question." Then the trembling boy began to sniffle; then he blubbered softly.

"Hold on," Father said firmly. "I'm not worried about your confession as much as I am about your confusion. You're mixing confession and confusion. Forget about this confession and see me at the rectory sometime next week. We'll figure out what dezgration is. Enough said. Enjoy your summer. Go in peace!"

Outside the confessional and much relieved, the boy started to run out of the church. Mrs. Twenter, however, caught him and whispered," Say your penance before you leave or you'll forget it." Gig knelt and said his penance from the earlier confession and then speeded home because the family was going to Jefferson for a movie. He didn't want to be late for that!

"Did you get lost?" his mother asked. "Hurry up! We're going to be late! Take a sandwich with you in the car!" Gig was grateful that her concern to get going excused him from questions about his return to church. He didn't want to cover up anything else. That bone wrapped in a gunny sack under the back porch was going to haunt him for awhile. K-Oats!

OPINIONS

Jefferson was halfway to Kansas City and Richard and his mother met the Bauers there before the movie, transferred Richard's suitcase to the Bauer car, and then all, except Phil, went to see Abbott and Costello. Phil wanted to get back to Kansas City before dark, so she and her Buick were there before the movie was over. After the movie, when they were getting ready for bed, Gig told Richard about dezgration and wanted him to see Father Boniface with him.

"We have to work together," he said to his cousin.

"Won't he be upset if we're talking about your confession? That's supposed to be none of my business."

"Well, he can tell us if that's the case. But you ought to know about dezgration too."

"I guess," Richard agreed with kind of a confused trust.

"Let me do the talking with Father," Gig volunteered.

Then the boys launched into other topics, which mostly revolved around Richard's experiences in the city. And, sooner than they planned, they were asleep and then called to get up. The next day, being Sunday, the boys went to mass with the family and spent most of the day greeting relatives and friends who made it point to visit with the Bauers as sabbatical enjoyment.

On Sunday evenings, as a rule, Grandpa Bauer and some of his friends made music with the piano, guitar, and mandolin. The women sat in the kitchen and exchanged recipes and news.

Grandma Bauer had letters from the Sisters who had received their package and a letter from Albert, mostly censored, but thanking everyone for mail, money, and prayers. Somehow the Bauer home was a place for more than a few to expand their horizons. The Sisters wrote about what they were learning during summer classes and Albert managed to furnish insight into oceanography and tropical flora and fauna.

On Monday morning, the boys only used 45 minutes for breakfast and weeding. Their grandfather had planned to take them fishing after his nap which followed every lunch. So the late morning was Gig's opportunity to take Richard to St. Hilda's rectory. Off the porch they flew after combing their hair.

"Where are you going?" Gen asked, interrupting her dress-making. Gen's income was the result of her skill as a seamstress, which had been perfected during her sojourn in Arkansas.

"It's a secret," Gig said laughing. They were down the

street and out of Gen's range when she said," Be that as it may, make sure you're here for lunch."

On the way to the rectory, Gig said," I've found this new way of keeping secrets. You say,' It's a secret.' and no one bothers you about it. And you don't have to lie."

At the rectory, Father Boniface acted like he didn't know why the boys had come so it seemed to Gig. He was sanding an old desk and handed each boy a strip of sand paper. As they worked, they talked. The priest learned a bit about Richard and they spoke about people they both knew in Kansas City.

The Gig blurted his frustration. "Can we talk about dezgration?" He then related all the elements about the bush whackers, the bone, his mother's definition of dezgration, and his slants and opinions.

The priest marveled at Gig's imagination but he was intrigued about the history involved.

"I think the bone must just be an animal's," Father stated.

"Can't be," said Gig diligently sanding.

"Well, why not?"

"Why would anyone wrap it to bury it?"

"Well..." the priest lagged thoughtfully. His imagination started to ignite.

Then Richard spoke up. "Do you think the Hubers butchered the bushwhackers? Is that why the bone is separated?"

Boniface tried to be very rational but he didn't know what to say for a few moments.

"Let's not let our imaginations go too far." Boniface loved a good story but he didn't treat Martin Meyer's information too lightly.

"Boys, this may turn out to be an eternal mystery and I don't know what more could be discovered."

Richard spoke up again. "Why does Grandma call that place 'The Boneyard?' She said it as plain as day."

"I'll ask her if you want," the priest declared.

"NO!" both boys yelled in unison. Then, more quietly, they said," No, Father."

"Where do we start on this mystery?" the priest questioned out loud though talking to himself.

"You'll help us then?" Gig said. "But you'll keep the secret, right?" he almost demanded.

"Yesss," the priest said slowly, still thinking of the interesting clues the boys had already gathered.

"What about me hiding the bone?" Gig asked. "Is it dezgration?"

Boniface explained desecration and made them practice saying the word properly. Then he said," Bring me the bone. I'll have it analyzed at the university hospital at Columbia. I have a friend who is a pathologist there. And don't frown like that. He will be verrry confidential. Just like a priest in the confessional." (Boniface did not think the bone in question could be human.)

"This way we'll know if you've found part of a bushwhacker." For the boys' sake, he did not smile.

Then Boniface hit upon another idea. "Why don't we go to Booneville and check on the old newspapers? Maybe we'll get some clues from them." Being a Benedictine monk, he knew that archives were full of interesting information. "Miss Dietrich will help us. When do you think this killing happened?"

"I don't know exactly but Grandma's dad was a boy on the Huber farm," Gig informed the priest.

The priest dusted himself off and left the back porch of his residence and headed for his office. "Keep sanding and don't gouge the wood," he said over his shoulder.

While he was gone, Richard looked over the desk while his cousin was biting his tongue and sanding away. Richard's finger was running over some of the slats which provided the pigeon holes and noticed one was loose. He pulled on it gently and out it came. A groove was exposed and in it a small piece of paper. Richard took his pocket knife and extracted a $100 bill!

Gig saw it! "WOW! WOW! Wow!" both screamed.

The priest came running and when he saw the bill, he joined in the dance around the desk. Then he declared," You guys are going to be detectives. You should be! Mysteries fall in your laps! This money, wherever it came from, is going to pay some bills this month. Alleluia!"

Then, acknowledging the boys' role in the discovery, he added:

"But some of it is going to pay for a great lunch in Booneville before we go to the library and look at the papers for 1865."

"Why 1865?" Richard asked.

"Because in 1865, Henry Huber was seven years old. Old enough to remember bushwhackers. I checked his age in the parish register. And because bushwhackers were most numerous toward the end of the Civil War. Furthermore, they would have been raiding in the summer or fall because harvests were available. That's what I think. We've narrowed things down a bit. Gosh! You kids make life interesting!"

Both boys beamed, intent on their adventure, more than on the compliment. Only the man who faced bill collectors knew the thrill he really needed.

"O.K. We'll go for lunch on Thursday. I'll tell your folks that I want you to help me with a project. We'll take your grandpa too but he'll lose us to visit his friends at the courthouse and at Pete's Cafe. I know him like a book."

Jessica Dietrich had a stack of bound newspaper on her desk when the trio of conspirators arrived at the library.

"Father, don't let these boys tear any of these pages or the three of you will be in the daily paper tomorrow and so will I for shooting you."

The priest spread the large book's pages on a table and started to go through headlines.

"While I read headlines, both of you scan the pages

for words like Huber, Bauer, German, and bushwhackers."
So they began.

Minutes became hours. A few columns spoke about German farm families. Marriages.

Baptisms. Funerals.

"Wait! Look here! " cried Richard. The headline read BUSHWHACKERS HARASS LOCAL FARMERS. The article didn't help much with details but it gave all of them greater hope for better information.

Miss Dietrich came over and wanted to know what was so exciting.

"Oh, nothin'," said Gig, trying to act more adult.

"They're looking up information about the Hubers and the Bauers," the priest told the librarian. "Boys, Miss Dietrich can really be helpful."

The boys looked at her, looked at the priest, and then shook their heads no. They understood what he was proposing and wanted no more conspirators.

"Hmmm," the librarian hummed to herself and disappeared, while the three detectives continued scanning pages of the brittle and brown newspaper. Then, the priest almost shouted. "Listen!" he said to the two who were already listening:

THREE VILLAINS DISAPPEAR AFTER RAID
THROUGH DEUTSCH COUNTY.

The two boys flanked the priest and almost crawled onto the table. Under the headline, they read together:

The three so-called rebels who have been
terrorizing Mid-Missouri have not been reported
to the authorities for over two weeks. Horses,
harvests, and women-folk appear to be saved
from the bloody hands of the three men believed
related. It is also believed that the three
have moved to the Great Plains and must be
harassing travellers and settlers there. We do
not wish the trio well.

"Gosh!" Richard said. "Doesn't that sound like our bones?"

"Could very well be," the priest replied. "But let's look for more clues."

Sure enough, on a day a few weeks later, the old paper read:

Still no sightings of the three pillagers. Report
any news of them to the Deutsch County sheriff.

"Would the Hubers have reported what they did, if they did," Gig inquired.

"Maybe not," the priest answered. "Remember they were not here long from Germany and they may not have wanted any shadow over their new citizenship."

"Did they commit murder, Father?" Richard asked.

"Not if they were defending themselves and their property. If they had gone broke from losses, their very lives were in danger. Those were chaotic times."

"K-Oats," Gig said under his breath.

"Let's keep going," their pastor urged. "And let's hope your grandpa found some long-winded drinking buddies."

"Why don't we go back to 1864? Maybe the gang will be mentioned for what they did before their disappearance."

"Good idea, Gig," the elder said. "Leave no stone unturned."

"I knew I remembered reading about the Huber name," Jessie spoke up suddenly from behind them, while toting another album of old newspapers. "Look at this." She removed her thumb as a maker and showed them an obituary column: YOUNG HUBER BURIED was the headline. In the article dated 17 March 1867, the paper described the requiem mass for and burial of Clement Huber, who had died as a result of gangrene.

"He died of blood poisoning," Boniface declared. "Two years after the disappearance."

"What disappearance?" the librarian asked.

"We can't explain right now, Jessie, We're still confused ourselves."

"Are you a Huber?" the librarian asked Richard.

"Our grandma is," both boys answered.

"Aren't many Hubers around here," she observed. Then an elderly lady called the librarian over to check out some novels.

The three searchers were stymied. Interesting information. Nothing clear.

"I still say it's called a "boneyard" for good reason," Richard asserted," and Grandma must know the varmits are buried on the old place. Father, why don't you talk to her? Ask her!"

"Let's get more information first. I still have to get the bone tested. But I'm in a bigger hurry than I was before."

"What will happen if Grandma knows about a murder?" questioned Gig.

"Curb the imagination, Boy," said the priest surely while his own mind was racing with curiosity.

ABSOLUTION

"**B**lood poisoning was terrible then," Jessie said, returning to the group." Very often the infection won. Thank God for the discovery of penicillin."

"How did you know Huber was in that particular book?" the priest asked the librarian.

"A family was here from Jefferson working on their family tree. They were looking through the 1867 newspapers. Not for Huber. I saw Huber and said to myself," Are there still Hubers in the county?" Librarians think like that. We make good detectives. But if you can't tell me your secrets, I can't help you."

"Boys?" the priest questioned.

Gig spoke. "If you swear her to secrecy."

The priest winked at the other adult. "Miss Dietrich can you keep a secret?"

"Oh, yes!" she smiled. "And if I can't, you will have to absolve me." The boys were not aware that some adult humor was being traded. Their language sounded official.

"Well, then. Here are the pieces of the story..." The priest went on to tell what they knew, what they imagined, what they found, and what they hoped to find.

Jessie sat down. "Wow! " she exclaimed. "This is going to be fun!" No one yet had said it was going to be fun. "I feel just like Nora Charles." (Nora Charles was the attractive wife of a famous movie detective.) Jessie fluttered her eye eyelashes.

"Habeas corpus?" Jessie asked the priest.

"Huh?"

"Father, don't you know your Latin or the law? Have you found the body or the bodies?"

"No bodies but the bone."

"Just one?"

"Yes, but I'm not sure that it's human."

The boys watched the librarian and the priest as though they were witnessing a tennis match.

"Let's dig up the boneyard," the librarian proposed. "I love archaeology." She did too.

"But first, get the bone tested in Columbia by a pathologist. Nobody but a pathologist."

"Right!" the priest said. "I have it in the trunk of my car but I can't get to Columbia today. I have to take these boys home. And their grandfather."

"I'll take the guys home. I want to see the site."

"Wait!" Richard said. "Grandpa will ride with us. We still have lunch to eat. You can't tell Grandpa! We're moving too fast!"

"Tell you what. Let's go eat now. Miss Dietrich can call a pathologist for me. She can take you to Wallenhorst when she closes the library while I'm in Columbia. After she drops you off, she can drive to the country by the old place. Right? Wait! What about your gasoline ration, Jessie?"

"I never go anywhere out of Booneville. I need an adventure!" piped "Nora Charles."

So the boys and their pastor had a fine meal at The Steak House. A feast of hamburgers and malts. The three of them must have spent most of three dollars counting the tip! The boys then returned to the library to delve and to wait for their grandfather. They decided to wade through the 1866 papers. Up and down the columns, four eyes ran like rabbits.

"Here's something!" Gig said once:
New priest in Wallenhorst. Father Michael of
Maria Monastery has taken over the duties of
Father Ludolph at St. Hilda's Parish.

Richard wrote it down in case it helped. He didn't think it would. The boys decided to check the headlines in 1864, feeling they needed to know more about the bush-whackers and they started with December and worked backwards.

"Try harvest time," Jessie said and they turned to August, September, and October. In early November they found:
Three Scourge Deutsch County
The reporter said that 3 young men resembling one another were posing as Confederate soldiers and threat-

ening farmers for the sake of horses, money, and food. The article continued to say that the Germans were reluctant to make trouble with the villains.

"If they got their belly full of violence and no one helped them," the librarian proposed,

"I could see some of them apply the law of survival." She explained what she meant. "I'd have blown their heads off in a minute! Enough is enough!" Jessie didn't seem like the usual librarian.

"Let's check 1865 once more before Grandpa gets here," Richard encouraged--now on fire with enthusiasm. Thanks to the librarian mostly.

Jessie clacked her chewing gum. She thought. Her teeth were like pistons. Then something caught her eye.

Mrs. Hale Visits County on a Search
This is what continued below the headline:

Mrs. Arthur Hale visited Booneville recently in an

attempt to find her 3 sons, Levi, Jacob, and Joseph, whom she claims are part of a lost regiment of the CSA. Mrs. Hale does not seem to be a lady of propriety, as her first visit was Gilliland's Tap outside Wallenhorst.

If her "boys" are the missing scavengers, we hope the lady from the Ozarks will leave before she is too greatly disappointed with the futility of her search. (Ed.s)

A little afterwards, Grandpa Bauer appeared in the library and was informed by Miss Dietrich that Father Boniface had a consultation with a doctor in Columbia. At 10 minutes after 4:00 P.M., the librarian shooed away two other grade schoolers. Girls! Then she locked the door and became the chauffeur for the three gentlemen.

It turned out that she had been in high school with the boys' Uncle Albert before her family moved to Booneville just prior to the War. She knew the other Bauers somewhat including the nuns. Miss Dietrich and Grandpa Bauer talked about old folks all the way to Wallenhorst.

"Understand your wife was a Huber."

"Yep," the elder replied. "Probably the last around here."

"Where was she reared?" Jessie questioned innocently. She was told. She had other questions too. And when the three "men" went into the house, Grandpa said he'd never heard anyone ask so many questions. But he figured librarians had to know a lot.

Jessie drove out to the Huber Place, which is what it was still called. She stopped at the house, introduced herself to Felicia, and accepted some iced tea. She asked Felicia if bookmobile services were to her satisfaction despite the wartime restrictions. Then she asked about local history. She went on to ask about the age of the farm buildings.

Felicia didn't know for sure. Jessie didn't gather much information at all. She was able to figure out where the boneyard was because she noted the large stones which seemed to be stored in the lot. Felicia didn't know about their origins; she guessed they were always there. One was flat on the ground. Three stones seemed to rise a bit above the ground like...

"...tombstones." Jessie said quietly.

Felicia laughed. "You've got quite an imagination, Jessie. You know we couldn't have a cemetery here. Catholics have to be buried in consecrated ground."

Jessie laughed too. She did not want Felicia to think she was snooping. She waved friendly as she drove away, just as the tractor bearing Paul turned into the driveway. He waved with the friendliness of the average farmer, glad to see company if not to talk to them. Felicia told him about the bookmobile survey.

"Bless me, Father, for I have sinned," Jessie said when Father Boniface's call reached her that night. "I pretended one interest while interested in something else. What did you find?"

"It is a human bone."

"No!" the librarian gasped.

"Probably a century old or thereabouts. A young man's bone according to your Doctor Hughes. He assumed I found it in our cemetery and I didn't correct him."

"Bless you, Father, and have you sinned?" Jessie laughed. She told him about the rest of the day, about the article about the Hale woman, about her questions to Mr. Bauer and Felicia, about seeing the stones. "My feminine intuition tells me that there are skeletons in the barnyard."

The priest ummed. "It seems to me that the Hubers and their descendants have inherited a mystery that is beyond them but in their backyard. And I'm not sure where to go with it."

"Did the doctor keep the bone?"

"No. I have it and I assured him that I would bury it again. He is so overworked, he could care less for a 100 year old bone. He probably wishes he had time for mysteries. I hope that I am not interrupting your duties, Jessie."

"I would have never forgiven you if you hadn't drawn me into this case. Librarians love this kind of thing. Of course, I have to do more digging. And, don't worry, mum's the word."

"I think I'd better thrash this business with Rose Bauer. The boys won't keep this secret much longer. They've already pulled in two of us in as many days. I'll keep you posted."

"And vice-versa."

That night, while the priest recited Compline, he prayed as usual for a quiet night and a peaceful death. He could not but think of restless souls and prayed for all of them too.

Jessie mused about the Huber yard before she fell asleep. "Why was the bone detached?"

she asked herself. "Was there butchery in addition to self-defense. Wow!" She loved mysteries and mayhem.

She hoped she could be Nora Charles in a dream that night and solve the case. But a side of her hoped she wouldn't...yet.

The boys had permission to stay up a little later that night and ate a great deal of popcorn. Hot buttered popcorn. Just like at the movies! And they listened to Grandpa Bauer's gossip from Booneville. Father Boniface had told the family about the boys finding the money and all were glad that St. Hilda's financial problems eased a bit. So much story telling distracted Rose and all went to bed without her remembering to sprinkle them with holy water. Unfortunately!

GHOSTS

Gen was having trouble falling asleep. Joe had asked her to marry him that evening and wanted to name a date. They had gone for a ride. He had stopped the car to look out over Buffalo Prairie. Then he told her that he wanted to be with her forever and that it was time for her and Gig to move out of Bauer house. She didn't tell him no but she asked for a week to think about it very seriously. The weight of his urgency and the decision she had to make finally pushed her down the aisle.

She was walking toward the altar but she was dressed black. Her father's arm felt like it was locking her, chaining her to him. She looked to the right. No one sat on the groom's side. Where were Joe's relatives? She looked to the left. Her sisters were there. Yes, even Mary and Ida were there, wrapped in their habits. Her mother was crying. The Sisters had their veils over their faces. Were they crying too? Phil was crying. She looked at Father Boniface in front of the altar. He was sour or maybe he was crying. He was flanked by his servers, Gig and Richard, who were both sobbing.

"Poor Joe!" she thought. "They shouldn't do this to him. It's such a special day for him." She looked for her groom; he was facing the altar but as she came to the end of the aisle, the groom turned. He was crying too. It was Randy! And his tears were blood. Then his face became a naked skull!

Gen screamed! She screamed! She screamed again! In fact, when she sat up in bed and realized she had been dreaming, she was still screaming. Then she realized that the boys in their bedroom next door were screaming.

When she got into Gig's room, her parents had already started up the stairs. As the light went on, a shrill cry came out of Gig who was standing against the headboard. Richard was on the floor half under the bed sobbing. Gen was grateful for her parents' entry. Her father grabbed the shrieking boy on the bed and held him in a firm but gentle embrace and her mother crawled on the floor beside Richard stroking him and cooing assurances. Gen sat on the boys' bed, wondering to herself if Randy's ghost had attacked them. Despite the excitement, she was not quite awake.

Rose finally hauled Richard onto the bed and then sat next to her daughter. In fact, the five of them packed the bed like survivors of a shipwreck. Rose looked at the scattered bed clothes and pillows and then at her shaken family. She broke the sounds of sniffling and murmurs. " This room looks like the Wreck of the Hesperus! Let's straighten it up. The boys acted like zombies and let the adults tuck them in and wait on them. Their grandfather brought them some grape juice, which he had "doctored" downstairs. The wine would rest them he figured

The women stroked the boys' hair and promised that the lights would stay on and Gen assured them that she wouldn't leave the room that night. She insisted, however, that her parents retire but they made her promise that she would sleep late next morning before they left her.

This time, Grandma splashed everyone, including herself, with holy water. "Nightmares weren't unheard of in the Bauer house but that night took the cake," Emil Bauer would declare later.

As the boys and Gen sipped their "grape juice", she asked them wisely if they needed to talk about their dreams. She laughed softly. "Since you entertained each other, you might as well entertain me." Both boys had had a nightmare, apparently simultaneously. Richard, at this point, was the calmest so he started:

"I was walking down the road by the Huber Place. Everything was gray and misty. Then a horse and buggy came down the road—toward me. The horse stopped and an ugly old lady leaned out of the buggy and shouted at me.

'You know where my boys are! You know where my boys are!'"

Gig gasped. "Mrs. Hale!"

"What?" asked Gen.

"Nothing," her son responded. Then to his cousin he said," What else?"

"I told her I didn't know her boys. 'What's their names?' I asked her. 'Death! Death! And Death!' she screamed at me. I said, ' Do they all have the same name?' "They're in the same shape!' she whined. Then I heard a voice wailing, 'Mama! Mama!' I looked on the other side of the buggy and there was a skeleton, trying to climb in her buggy. But he didn't have all his bones. Then another skeleton came. And it had the same problem. Couldn't get in the buggy. Not enough bones to climb. Than it happened to a third skeleton the same way.

The old lady kept trying to pull the skeletons in the buggy but they kept falling into the ditch that looked like a grave it was so deep. Finally, she got angry and screamed at me again.

'This is your fault! This is their fault! You'll pay! I'll be back!' She took her whip and hit the horse so hard it kicked and caught me with its hoof and I went in the air, screaming because I was heading for the ditch with those skeletons. I started screaming and crying until I opened my eyes and saw that I was with Grandma"

His aunt stroked Richard's hair again and told him it sure was a scary dream. She made him sip some more of the "grape juice." Then she turned to her son. "Honey, tell me about your dream." Then Gig started:

"I was looking for Daddy..."

Gen stiffened. But bravely she said, " Go on."

"I couldn't find him but I saw many soldiers. Some in blue uniforms. Some in gray. They were camped in the yard behind the Huber house. I kept asking for my dad but I didn't know what name to call him because I've always called him Daddy. Why don't I know his name, Mama?"

"We've always called him Daddy. Why don't you continue your dream?"

"Then I saw you helping a soldier. He was leaning on you. But you really weren't helping him because I saw he was strangling you. I wanted you to know I was there to help you so I shouted, 'Mama"! Mama!'"

"That was you!" Richard started.

"Huh?"

"Honey, go on."

"When I got closer to you I saw that soldier only had one leg. So I knew it would be easy to help you. I kicked him. I yelled at him. I told him that he would pay. And I told you I'd be back. I went to get a stick or club. I went to the barnyard and found a heavy white stick. It was shaped like a leg..." Gig stopped. He looked at Richard.

"Go on." Gen urged.

"I ran back to you," he said to his mom," and I started hitting the soldier with the bone, eh, the stick. He screamed. But I kept hitting him and kicking him hard."

"Me." said Richard.

Gig continued. "Then the man turned and looked at me with pain and he said, ' Do you want to know who I am?' Then Mama you screamed and I didn't hear who he said he was. Next he threw a bag over my head. It was dark and I thought I was his prisoner of war until the light came on and I saw that Grandpa was holding me."

Gen was truly shaken, though she smiled at the boys. She remembered her dream. Richard's dream didn't mean much to her except that Gig's dream ran into his cousin's. Gig's dream troubled her more than her own. She pulled him toward her for awhile. Her mother had left the familiar bottle on the nightstand and Gen rose and walked toward it. The cousins were whispering a conversation but they quieted when she sprinkled them again. All of them prayed for the souls of the dead, especially for Gig's daddy.

"What was Daddy's name?" Gig asked.

"His given name was Randall and soon I'm going to tell you much more about him. I promise. But I want both of you to sleep now." She had noticed Richard nodding ever so slightly. Gen nudged her son to the middle of the bed and she wrapped him with her right arm and invited him to sleep. "Sweet dreams," she murmured. "Richard, are you O.K., Honey?"

He did not answer. "Gig?" He only grunted softly.

She left the lamp on. It cast a comforting glow around the room. Its light fell on dirty socks and underwear. It fell on rocks and jars full of crawling worms and bugs. It fell on the crucifix on the wall. It fell on suitcases. It fell on a picture of the Hubers, perhaps taken 40 years ago, when Rose was a young woman leaning on her father, on Henry Huber, who was adored by his Rose. The lamplight held at bay the darkness which had tried to overtake the vulnerable woman and the innocent boys, all of whom slept the rest of the night with faces like angels.

EXORCISM

The morning after, Gen told her parents about the three dreams. They listened in dead quiet during her telling and kept quiet afterwards as though they were thinking hard about directions which needed to be followed. Their muted activity around the breakfast table enabled the boys upstairs to sleep longer. A few times, Rose started to speak but it was as if her mind had not yet given her mouth permission to speak. After her account of the previous night, Gen went silent too, so that the three of them were each separated from the others, from the kitchen, from the house. Each drifted, almost praying, definitely reviewing the past while considering the future. Finally, Gen spoke up. "I'm telling Gig about Randy today."

Her father questioned doing so after such a rough night. "Wait a day or two, Gen," he suggested.

"Definitely," her mother added. Then said it again. "Definitely."

"Mom, what about this business of the boneyard?"

Rose replied. "Some of the information baffles me. In fact, most it does." The tone of her voice was honest in its confusion.

"Dad?"

"I'm no good at interpreting dreams. I don't know how important dreams are. But I would say these are important. Almost evil."

"The boneyard has got to go," Rose muttered to herself but aloud. Her husband and daughter heard.

"What do you mean, Honey?" Emil asked.

"I mean that the business needs to be aired. Ever since I was little, I was told not to talk about the boneyard but I didn't know what there was about it and why there was a secret. All of us were almost sworn to a secret but didn't know what the secret was. Bones, I thought, meant skeletons. So I thought, as I got older, instead of having skeletons in our closet, they were in our backyard. I never grasped the idea of skeletons, as much as the importance of family secrets, however."

"Is that why you always shush stories about the bushwhackers and the early Hubers?"

Gen inquired.

"Yes, but I don't plan on doing it any longer. Watching those boys last night and listening to you this morning convinces me. And..."

Before Rose could say more, the phone jangled and, since she was the nearest to it, she answered. "Hello, Bauer residence.

Good morning, Father.

Yes, we'll be around this morning. The boys are still sleeping but...

No, we don't mind letting them stay in bed for awhile.

Half an hour? Fine.

Goodbye.

God bless you too."

When Rose hung up, she told the others that Father Boniface wanted to deal with something and would be there soon. Gen ran for the bathroom to dress and to primp because, unlike her parents, she was not quite ready to face the day. After ten minutes in the bathroom, she tiptoed up the stairs to put on a fresh blouse and skirt. And by the time the priest arrived, the coffee table was ready to host him and the Bauers were gathered in the front room.

Just before he made the three minute drive to the Bauers, the pastor's phone rang and he took a call from a cheery Jessie Dietrich.

"I found out the owner of the leg," she declared.

"What ?"

"I've figured out why that bone was alone."

"How?"

"The old papers. Listen to this:

DOCTOR VON DER AHE PERFORMS AMPUTATION.

I overlooked that headline, forgetting that in 1867 in rural Missouri amputations would have been exciting news. I'll go on with the article:

```
A young farmer of the Wallenhorst community
lost his right leg in a surgery three days ago at
his family's farm. It is hoped that Clement
Huber, suffering from gangrene, will profit from
this procedure.
```

"That's it!" the priest exclaimed. "That's where the leg came from! Jessie, Nora Charles would be so proud of you. I'll get back to you soon but I have to run now. Keep sleuthing. And thanks a million!"

In a few minutes, the pastor was in the Bauer's living room, expressing his concern for the complications arising from Gig and Richard's curiosity. Completely unaware of what the Bauers needed to discuss with him, he proceeded to tell them what he knew about the boneyard.

"I went along with them to prove that their imaginations were too active. But the papers from that time have proved their imaginations valid."

The Bauers looked at each other and squirmed.

The priest told them about Jessie's call related to the amputation. (He had already told them about the bone which Gig and Richard had extracted from the barnyard.) "I'm concerned, nevertheless, that this business could boil over," he concluded.

"It has." Emil spoke up. Then the Bauers told their part of the dramatic developments.

The priest already knew about Gig's paternity and Gen's secret, so he was not taken aback by her information. In fact, he wondered to himself about the dreams being spiritual messages to surface "skeletons" (secrets) so that they could be properly considered. He listened to Gen's proposal to inform Gig of his background and he agreed with her but also with her father's suggestion about timing. He was curious about the boneyard but Rose could only say that she was a custodian (as a Huber) of a family secret.

"I've thought seriously about the bushwhacker business," Boniface continued. "It would be a good idea to call the Missouri State Historical Society, inform them of the present information, and let them take over. Of course, Paul and Felicia would have to permit exhumations and whatever." The four of them "knew" the bushwhackers would be found under the mysterious stones. Each had an active scenario in his/her imagination.

"I can't see any trouble involving the Historical Society," Emil said.

"After last night's production," Rose said," I'd dig the bones up myself. But," she stressed," the boys cannot be present if there is a disinterment." She declared herself infatically.

"I think it's about time for Gig to visit his dear aunt in Kansas City. We'll find out if there's going to be grave digging and that's when he going to be in Kansas City with his cousin, getting a dose of city life," Emil declared.

All nodded in assent. By that time, Gig would profit from the electrical antics of his Aunt Phil. All of them smiled when they thought of her entertaining Gig.

Then Gen introduced another topic. A related topic. "Father, what do you think of me marrying Joe Schuster? He needs an answer."

Her parents were not surprised at the proposal. Neither was the pastor. He replied without any hesitation. "It's about time. Joe needs a good wife. You need a good husband. And your son needs a father."

"He's had a good father," Gen responded, looking at her dad.

"He's had a GRAND father. GRAND! Absolutely grand. But you know what I mean. Besides, let's give your father a break. He may not be so grand if he has to raise another teenager.

"I never thought about THAT!" the older man laughed.

The priest spoke to Gen's parents. What do you think of Joe's proposal?"

Rose spoke up. "Even if Gen didn't care for Joe, I'd be tempted to pay her to marry him."

"So many people are involved in this proposal," Gen intervened. "I didn't want to put myself first."

Her father walked over to her and kissed the top of

her head. "That's why Joe loves you so much: You love so much."

The priest accepted a homemade donut from Rose. About then, all of them looked at the ceiling because there were light footsteps on the bedroom floor above them.

"Will it be hard on Gig to hear what Gen has to tell him," Rose asked the men.

Emil answered first. Smaller children are wiser than teenagers. I think he can deal with it well now. What do you think, Father?"

"I don't think Gen should tell him bluntly. You can orchestrate it, can't you,Gen?

Last night, all of you dealt with shadows together. Before long, shed light on the situation together. Both boys will need to hear the secrets because they are soul mates, as if you didn't know. Who do you think will be discussing this with Gig for the most part. It won't be you or I."

"Father, we can't thank you enough for your part in clearing this mess," Rose said gratefully. You're a good exorcist."

"It's not really a mess," the priest replied. "There's a goodness operating here. It's as though Truth wants to assert itself for the sake of all of us. And," he chuckled," we have to thank some folks who fed the boys fiction and facts. Somehow both fit together for the boys to produce a solution. Jessie Dietrich deserves a great deal of thanks for solving a major portion of the mystery of the single bone."

"What are you going to do with that thing?" asked Emil.

"This afternoon I'll be in the cemetery with a shovel and digging in Clement Huber's grave, deep enough to return his leg to him. The rest of the village will be absorbed in their own work. How does that set with you, Rose?"

"It's fine with me only if Emil can help you, Father. Someone from the family with you, you know."

"Father, will you tell the boys about the leg?" Gen requested.

"Tell us what?" a raspy voice spoke as Gig entered the front room, followed by a fellow spectre with hair awry, slitted eyes, and growling innards.

THE WITNESS TREE

"Richard. Grandma has some chairs she wants you to set up out by the boneyard," Gen told her nephew, while she and her son stood in the shade of the thick old tree by the ancient road to Wallenhorst which drifted by the Huber Place. It was a tree they treasured. It had shaded that spot long before Rose was born and, according to her, her father had swung on it and in it as a boy.

"What's going on in the barnyard?" Gig asked cautiously. His eyes were wide and glancing, looking for activity.

"Your grandma's going to give us all a talking to. Even your Aunt Phil is on her way here. By the way, she wants to take you to Kansas City for two weeks so you can see what's going on in other parts of the world."

That information made Gig wonder and, while he was his wondering, his mother clasped his hand and led him down the road in the direction of Clear Creek. "Let's take a little walk, Gig."

They strolled by the wide fields high with brilliant green vegetation meant for animals and humans. They watched a hawk looking for lunch. They laughed at two dung beetles and chided them for working so hard on a Sunday. The day was perfect. Not too hot but warm enough to feel the perspiration of Mother Nature, holding the mother and son, who blended so well in her creation.

"I want to talk to you about your father, Gig." Gen managed to be so calm that Gig made no display of surprise.

"Good," he responded evenly. "I feel like I should know more about him. I don't trust dreams to show him to me."

"I'm going to tell you some things about your father now," Gen started," but some other things will have to wait until you're older. In fact, there is much that even I don't know about him."

"He was killed in the war, right?"

"Yes, but not early in this war like I led you to believe. As a matter of face, he was killed recently."

"Will we go to the funeral?" Gig asked with curiosity not grief. Not have his father's acquaintance gave him a kind of detachment Gen supposed. She hedged.

"He's already buried, Gig."

"Can I see his tombstone?"

"Maybe when you're older. But let me tell you some things you should know about first of all. To start, your father was not my husband. I was not his wife."

"How can that be?"

Two red-wing blackbirds were calling to each other.

"Well, sometimes a man and a woman can have a

child by just getting too close to each other with their bodies and their feelings."

"Like bulls and cows?" Gig asked innocently, with a knowledge she should have planned on but didn't.

"Well," she drawled," not exactly but I suppose you're on the right track when it come to understanding copulation."

"Is that a word I should memorize?"

A colt ran up to the fence to investigate them. Somewhere the mare whinnied.

"Why not?" Gen laughed. "But let me continue. Your father and I were close friends before he went to war."

"And his name was Randall," Gig chimed.

"Correct. Gig, please let me talk without interruption. Randall and I never thought about getting married and, as a matter of fact, we never thought about a lot of important things period. Before we knew it, we had gotten too close to each other. Closer than people should be unless they're married. The next thing I knew I was pregnant with you." She paused.

Gig said,"I know what pregnant means." as he tossed a rock at a red-wing.

"O.K. Anyway...your father was very young, a boy. About 16..."

"That's old!" Gig protested.

"Not old enough to be a good husband and father! Rand—, eh Randall got terrified and ended our friendship then and there. I never talked to him again after he learned that I was pregnant. He went to work for awhile in Kansas City. And I went to Fort Smith to finish school while I waited for you to appear."

"It took me nine months."

"Right. You're quite a scientist, aren't you? Gig, why do you think I moved to Fort Smith?"

"To be close to the Sisters?"

"Yes, so you and I would both have good care. But also to keep my pregnancy a secret until it was over. I didn't want a bunch of questions about having a baby without having a husband, you know?"

"People are nosy...like me," the boy admitted.

"Well, I wanted you to know that your father was a boy who could not be a good father to you but I don't want you to think badly of him. Teenagers are crazy. We both did crazy things, like getting too close."

"Will I be a crazy teenager?"

"Very! Very! Very!" his mother stressed and then hugged him. "But I will always love you. Just take to heart what I mean about being too close when distance is the best thing."

"Like the bull and the cow?"

"Well, yes, if you really want to use that example. Where did you...?"

"I watch."

"Um." Gen was drained. She was relieved when she and her son heard the dinner bell ringing at the farm house.

"As you get older, I want to talk about this subject again. Not all at once. It's too much to digest all at once. And, " she added, " it's something that only the family discusses. Don't forget that."

"I wonder what Grandma wants to talk about."

"Is that on your mind too?"

"Gosh, yes!"

"What I really want to know is if you took what I have just been saying to heart."

"I will, sooner or later, because I have to sort it out. Can I talk to Richard about it?"

"You can talk to any of our close family about it but that's all...except for Father Boniface. He has to keep secrets. One other thing. Maybe more important." The bell rang again. Gen grasped her son's shoulders and looked into his dark brown eyes.

"I need a husband and I think you could use a father. And I know just the man."

"Joseph Schuster. Let's go or Grandma will holler at us!"

"Wait!" Gen caught him as he started to run. "You figured this out already?"

"Two years ago! Do you think I'm blind? You're tired of being fallow. I like the idea. Will I have to be a Schuster? I like being a Bauer."

"Well," Gen answered," could you be Gregory Emil Bauer-Schuster?"

"Can I drop the 'Emil'?"

"NO!"

"O.K. Let's go!" The two of them ran toward the group in the yard with a grandmother, arms akimbo, looking a bit impatient. One of the dogs was barking for her.

In a few minutes, all were seated in lawn chairs or on benches or on the lawn nearest to the boneyard under the wonderful old tree in its best shade. There was quiet when Rose Huber Bauer said, "O.K."

"Sometimes secrets are good," Rose began. "Sometimes they fester however, when the people who should know about them don't. That's one reason we go to confession. It's a reason we have fathers and mothers, husbands and wives, aunts and uncles, and bosom friends." Gig grinned at Richard. Rose's children were not accustomed to their mother's eloquence and they were making sure that their offspring were paying close attention as they were. Even Aunt Phil, who had just arrived, seemed serious. The dogs were running after something wild in the high grass across the road.

"When I was a girl," Rose continued," my father brought me right here and pointed to that patch there with the large stones and told me that no one should ever plow it, garden it, or doing anything with it other than mow it. He said it was a boneyard and that it was my duty to see to it that no one or no thing ever disturbed it. When I asked why he told me that it was a boneyard and that all I needed to know was what he told me to do. Paul will tell you that I passed the same directions on to him."

"Of course, I had suspicions because, even then, people like Virgil Kempchen and Martin Meyer talked a lot about bushwhackers and what not." Gig and Richard looked at each other expectantly. Rose went on. "Thanks to their tall talking and two grandsons who should be detectives, the boneyard is about to become a gift to science."

About four voices piped. "What?"

"I mean that we're going to find out if those three big rocks mark three graves. Oh, we're not going to dig them up. Some folks will be here this summer from the Historical Society and take charge. If the bushwhackers are there, it's finally time for them to leave. Somehow, they've managed to cause grief again.

Richard piped up. " We get to watch, right?"

His grandmother answered almost sharply. "I don't know when those folks will be here exactly. So I'm making no promises for a sideshow."

His grandfather added," We will keep all detectives informed."

Rose proceeded again. "Once or if they find the bushwhackers' bones, the Historical Society will help us piece the story together but they think there will be some gaps in the story if they find the bones. One of the folks has talked to me, Martin, and Virgil over the phone about the stories told by the old folks. One of the other folks from the Society has talked to Father Boniface about the German immigration to Missouri and has gone through old newspapers with Miss Dietrich at the Booneville library. I think we have three villains over there who died the way they planned to kill our ancestors. I feel their evil intentions in my bones even as I stand here with you."

There was some murmuring, especially among the youngsters. Gig and Richard were proud of their detective work but they were also sad that the "cat was out of the bag" as their grandmother said it.

"One thing I learned from this secret," Rose stated firmly, " is that families should share information like this instead of shushing and shishing like I've always done. My dad didn't feel the same way but he saw what we didn't and he and his family did not have the resources to deal with incidents as we do now. Be that as it may, we are going to use this boneyard as a barnyard again." Leaves on the tree with a breeze's motion seemed to applaud.

Felicia spoke. "I'd like to use it for an extension of the lawn and as a flower garden."

"Good idea!" Rose declared. "Good idea!"

"I have an idea too," Gen said standing. "Why don't we have my wedding party there next June?"

At that news, Phil squealed like a pig. Her nephews were injured by the pitch of her voice. Then they all laughed as she squeezed her sister like a lady wrestler would. Rose shook her head because of the unruly daughter but she smiled broadly. Emil Bauer walked over to the pair of young women and added a third to the hug. He was more affectionate than Rose, who preferred to show her strength more than her softness.

Gig and Richard were in a huddle during the excitement, talking about the "digs." They would be disappointed after the fortnight in Kansas City to discover that the bones had been under the stones and were gone awaiting reburial after some studies by professors. The boys would be present however when Father Boniface came to bless the spot with prayers and much sprinkling as Rose held the brass bucket full of holy water.

The boys would see the yard still scarred from digging but re-seeded with grass and displaying a few mums which Felicia transplanted. In a year they would read an article see their names in print. About the same time, they visited the three graves in a row at Mount Pisgah Cemetery. A stone, placed later, would state the theory about the brothers' intention and demise.

It was not long after the bones had been transferred to the new graveyard that Martin Meyer died and was buried in St. Hilda's Cemetery. "He was the last of the story tellers," Virgil Kempchen claimed but anyone who knew Virgil knew that he was Martin's worthy replacement.

In the fall following the summer excitement, Father Boniface had gone to his abbey and brought back a stone sculpture of The Holy Family and gave it to the Bauers for the "yard project." Paul and his sons built an attractive grotto to house the figures, using the three "grave stones" as part of its base. Felicia made sure that the earliest spring flowers would be there to decorate the scene. She planted beauty where once a terrified farmer had buried a savage family.

The family agreed to pray for the souls of the Hale brothers every November day.

But whenever their names were mentioned, Rose would say, " May they rest in peace. Amen."

Phil and Richard, Albert, and the Benedictine Sisters received black and white photographs of the grotto and went along with the new custom of calling the boneyard "The Grotto."

When Christmas came, Sergeant Fitzpatrick brought his bubbling wife to Wallenhorst along with their son, "The Sleuth", as he proudly called him. When Easter came, now Mister Fitzpatrick brought his very pregnant wife to Wallenhorst, who came to be measured for the dress of the matron of honor. When June came, Mr. and Mrs. Fitzpatrick came down the aisle of St. Hilda's, several steps ahead of a bride wearing a light blue dress and a mantilla of the same color. Gen was radiant on the arm of her father. Albert and the Benedictines were there in spirit as they each said in their long letters to her. In addition to Joe at the altar end of the aisle was Father Boniface, flanked by two acolytes, eager to end the mushy ceremony. No one had noticed that their fingernails were dirty. No one knew that they had another "project" in operation. No one paid them any attention as the wedding party danced around The Grotto and the tables loaded with food and drinks. And that suited the two boys under the maple tree just fine.

ABOUT THE AUTHOR

Gary Young, a Missouri native, joined the
International Resurrectionist community in 1971.
He was attracted by its educational ministry as a
way of elevating society's character. His professional
credentials are based on three graduate degrees:
Theology, English, Library Science.

Young's teaching career moved from Missouri to
Illinois, then to Kentucky where he taught secondary
and college levels. Since 1996 he has served the
headquarters of the Sister of Charity of Nazareth as
a priest. Presently, he lives a contemplative life in
rural Kentucky.

He is the author and illustrator of *Cactus
Spirituality, Pater Hilarion.*